REFLECTIONS
IN A
FADED MIRROR

short Short Stories
from the deep Deep South

REFLECTIONS IN A FADED MIRROR

*short Short Stories
from the deep Deep South*

Toretha Wright

Publisher's Note
This book is a work of fiction. Names, characters, places, and
situations either are used fictitiously or are products of the
author's imagination. *Shall We Gather at the River* was written
by Robert Lowry, 1864. Copyright status is Public Domain

Library of Congress Control Number: in-publication-data
Wright, Toretha, 1954-

ISBN: 978-1720476375
ISBN: 1720476373

Published by *WrightStufco*
_____
803-446-6096
www.wrightstuf.com

Printed in the United States of America

For now we see only a reflection as in a mirror; then we shall see face to face.

~1 Corinthians 13:12

I thank God for my blessings!

For my parents…

The Stories

The Gospel Deliverance Tent Revival

"Fornication! Fornication!"

Prophet Malachi Jenkins shouted through the microphone that carried his booming voice from the camp meeting ground through the muggy town streets. People jumped up and down. Some leaning backward with the privileged knowledge that others wouldn't let them fall. Old women - in bright multicolored dresses and gaudy straw hats, bare legs, and flat platformed sandals - stood on their feet with their hands waving in the air; big straw pocketbooks swinging in the bends of their arms. With eyes clenched shut, some peeped through the glistening sweat running down their eager faces, while shouting, "Hallelujah, Hallelujah! Thank you, Jesus," in high-pitched voices.

An assortment of old men stood or sat in the back of the large open tent with a few *amens* coming from only a few of them. Young children sat slumped in chairs - some hard asleep, some squirming around - not enjoying the hellfire and damnation sermon reverberating around them. Like the children, some men slept with their faces buried underneath brimmed hats that eventually slid down and landed on slow heaving chests.

Coleman snored easily with the pungent aroma of Miss Remer's scrap iron whiskey hovering around him. The extended duration of the service gave an understanding of how folks slept against the constant clanging of the tambourines and the alternating pounding of the big bass drum. James Junior stood up, stretching his legs and patting the wrinkles from his freshly pressed pants. He appeared ornery. It was almost midnight, and James Junior had to go to work early Friday morning. *I been up late every night this week,* he thought. *I be damned if I'm comin' out here tomorrow night.*

In reality, he wanted to go to Holiday's Beer Garden with the rest of the unsaved an unconvinced. Holiday's stood clear on the other side of town, but James Junior felt obliged to drive his Aunt Sophie to the annual Gospel Deliverance Tent Revival. It had been a duty ever since he learned how to drive. If he had left her there, his kinfolks would never let him live it down. Some already had said, "He's biggity – just too big for hisself - after Sophie done raised him when his own mama left him and went up north with the horses."

James Junior wasn't biggity, per se, but just trying to be a man in a house full of strong-minded women – sweet Aunt Sophie, who never married, and uppity Aunt Janie Mae, who left Uncle Man in Philadelphia years before and never went back. He didn't ask her to come back either, and they both seemed happier in spite of it. There was also a high traffic of girl cousins flowing in and out the house with their children of no-name fathers, who often made beds there, too. But they were family, and James Junior never minded the aggravation of family - sometimes.

The tent visitors were plenty that year even though it proved to be the hottest month Lambert ever had. The rain had abandoned the south for several weeks in a row. Folks counted their blessings nonetheless as the mosquitoes were scarce. The mosquito truck still made nightly rounds spraying up and down the streets while mothers and grandmothers called the children in from raucous play under the dim streetlights.

It had been a sad year, too. Martin Luther King, Jr. and Bobby Kennedy, both shot in the head. Folks had just stopped talking about John Kennedy and Malcolm X. Miss Sophie said it was a sour year and swore murders came in threes. She had everybody speculating who would be next. Most folks had said, Lyndon Johnson, since he'd signed that civil rights bill. "White folks still aint over that," she'd said. Others pondered over Adam Clayton Powell, Jr., but Sophie had just snickered and mumbled, "He done bout assassinated hisself already."

"Fornication is a sin," shouted Prophet Malachi. He leaped from the raised platform and strutted in front of the crowd of excited church folk, who were sitting (some standing) there swaying and waving their hands high in the air, shouting, "Hallelujah!"

Aunt Sophie yelled from one of the wooden chairs lined on the front row, "Bring it home, Prophet." There's gonna be some fornication tonight.

Coleman woke up and lamented a confused, "Amen."

Prophet Malachi hollered, "If you commit adultery, you have fornicated. Jesus went unto the Mount of Olives earrrrrrrly in the morning."

"Amen!" shouted some of the people, while others just rocked and nodded it.

Prophet Malachi pulled a hard-starched white cotton handkerchief from the breast pocket of his hard-starched beige linen suit. His processed graying hair dripped with sweat. "He came again into the temple, and all the people came unto him, and he sat down and taught them."

"Preach!" Someone yelled out from the back. The congregation's eyes followed Prophet Malachi as he paraded up and down the aisle that was just right for shouting and praying.

"And the scribes and Pharisees brought to him a woman." He paused and stared into the crowd. "I said a woman who was taken in adultery."

Sophie cried out, "Preach, Prophet."

"And when they had set her in the midst, they said unto him, Master." Prophet Malachi shouted, "I don't

4

think y'all heard me." He paused leaving the congregation waiting in suspense for a moment.

"Master," he continued softly. "This woman was taken in adultery, in the very act."

"Talk to me, preacher man," whispered another old woman from an aisle seat sitting sideways to see Prophet Malachi marching in glory.

"Now Moses in the law commanded us that such should be stoned."

"Hallelujah!" Aunt Sophie shouted with the others, but hers resonated high above the crowd.

"But what sayest thou?"

"Preach!" said one little boy, who by now sat wide-awake and rocking wildly in his chair.

Coleman sitting next to him added as he raised his head, "Preach, Rev!" He shifted his body in the hard-folding chair and again snored quickly.

Prophet Malachi preached hard. "Well! This they said, tempting him that they might have to accuse him! But Jesus stooped down. He stooped down, and with his finger wrote on the ground, and acted as though he heard them not! Can I get an Amen?"

"Amen! Amen!"

"Amen!"

Prophet Malachi reached his hand high into the air, "Can I get another Amen?"

The crowd shouted and stomped Amens.

"Amen, Prophet," hollered Aunt Sophie high above the crowd. "Amen!"

"So, when they continued asking him, he lifted up himself, and said unto them, He that is without sin among you!"

Prophet Malachi paused. The crowd waited. Verbally and physically like an image on a video, motionless, waiting; anticipating.

"AND JESUS SAID. HE THAT IS WITHOUT SIN AMONG YOU CAST THE FIRST STONE AT HER!"

As if the video pause button was released, the crowd reanimated in full motion with shouting and crying and laughing in joy from the sermon.

Miss Sophie launched into a progression of leaps and turns, shouting, "Hallelujah! Hallelujah." Her arms thrashed in the air excitedly as she shouted and shuffled in jubilation. James Junior's effort at restraining her went wanting. "All right, Aunt Sophie," he said in frustration. "You go on."

Her out-of-control swinging arms struck James Junior square in the nose. Hard. "Damn! Blood!" He clutched his nose with both hands. Through the excited crowd, someone passed him a handkerchief, while an usher woman pressed a cold, wet towel from an ice bucket on his nose. He held his head back. The bleeding didn't stop.

Coleman lifted his head from a slow nod. "Drop some cold keys down his back! That'll stop it," he said matter-of-factly.

The cold keys didn't stop the bleeding. James Junior figured the way to halt his nosebleed was to leave the heat of the crowded tent. "Coleman, tell my Aunt Sophie I'll be back ta git her."

"Alright," Coleman said, scratching nappy graying hairs in unkempt whiskers. "I'll tell her." Between nods, Coleman resumed the *Hallelujahs* and *Amens* with the rest of the congregation.

Soon after Miss Sophie calmed down, she fell back softly in her chair - out of breath – out of hallelujahs. The usher women fanned her down. She had been saved – again.

The gospel had been delivered. Souls were right, and the money had been collected. One more night of the gospel, then Prophet Malachi Jenkins would be gone once more - until next year.

"Need a ride home, Sophie?" Coleman asked, knowing that James Junior was at Holiday's with an ice-cold beer and probably a girl of notable distinction.

"No thank you, Coleman. James Junior will be back directly." Miss Sophie answered, agitated that he asked. She wasn't sure if James Junior would be back, but she didn't want a ride with Coleman in any case. There had been a time when she would have smiled at such an offer from Coleman. When there was something sweet between the two of them. Thirty years ago. When Coleman was somewhat sober and slightly handsome. When they both were young and vibrant. Thirty years later, Miss Sophie was still vibrant. Too vibrant for the likes of Coleman and his corn whiskey. At least this night.

Miss Sophie waited for James Junior at the back of the tent. Her damp cotton dress clung vividly to her form. She wiped sweat from her neck and the cleavage of her full bosom with a lace handkerchief from her pocketbook. Her long graying hair had fallen from the neatly pinned French bun, and she let it flow effortlessly on one shoulder.

Coleman looked around to see that Miss Sophie was the last congregate inside the large tent. "You sho you gon be alright, Sophie."

"Yes, Coleman, I said I'm gon be just fine. Goodnight." She hastily waved him away.

"Goodnight, Sophie." Coleman departed looking forward to another fifty cents shot of Miss Remer's smooth scrap iron whiskey.

Was it a sign? Sophie was alone now. Just her, the night, and Malachi Jenkins. The dimly lit tent masked the slow age lines and the eager anticipation on her face. It had been a year. She had waited. Once a year for three decades. The same town, the same man. Malachi walked deliberately towards her, sweat lingering on his forehead, "It's a sign," he grinned. "It's got to be a sign."

Sophie smiled broadly, as she took hold of his warm hand, "Yes! She proclaimed, "He who is without sin, let him cast the first stone."

Miss Lucy's Pie

Listen up! And I will tell you about Miss Lucy Jacobson and me. With her smooth skin and shapely figure, she never looked a day past thirty. Moreover, I had known her for nearly forty years. The humidity of the southern summer sun and the crisp cold winter air kept her looking young; so she said. Her daddy's people aged leisurely, but not like her. Most of them were teetotalers. But I have a story or two I could tell you about her brother, Henry, Lord, rest his soul. It seemed like every time someone spoke of that man they'd say just that, "Lord, rest his soul." Or shake their heads. The whiskey didn't kill him, though. It was Fred Morgan – for messing with his chickens. But that's another story.

Miss Lucy was what we southerners call a maiden lady since she was way up in age and never had a husband of her own. I'm not one to mix words, so don't expect me to sugar coat what I'm about to tell you.

Now, being a single lady or an old maid, as some folks called her, might call up a mental picture of an unattractive, childless, middle-aged sour woman. A woman who is just miserable, lonely, and living in other folks' shadows. Like she's someone to be pitied because she doesn't have a man to cook for and pick up after and get regular loving from whether she wants it or not. A woman who doesn't have a man to grow old with no matter how miserable he makes her feel. Wait a minute. I'm getting off the subject.

Well, Miss Lucy was none of that. She was all smiles and pleasantries. Reminded me of that movie star, Doris Day.

My family had worked for Miss Lucy and her family for the better part of my years. Miss Lucy was a nice enough girl growing up. Never got into trouble from what I can remember. When she graduated from Lambert High School years ago, her mama and daddy sent her upstate to this all girl's college where she studied geography. Nevertheless, she became a schoolteacher since that's what her mother wanted.

While she was in her college learning how to teach their children, my mama and daddy sent me to State College, so I could teach ours. I know her mama didn't like that I was leaving from cleaning up after them, so I could learn how to do something other than clean up after them. But my mama had dreams for us, too.

Miss Lucy came back to Lambert and taught at the same school from which she had graduated four years earlier. She remained there teaching the same class for years. That might sound like a dull existence to you, but it's the goings on in between the learning and the teaching, too that make life worthwhile. It's true; you cannot judge a book by its cover or by its title for that matter. You'd think someone with the name Lucy Jacobson was some kind of dull.

Miss Lucy wasn't such a good cook, except for her lemon pies. I don't mind telling you that when she poured a lemon pie, I could hardly wait until it chilled. Those pies were special. Also, I'd let her know her pie making was a gift, by how my hips grew.

Anyhow, she taught school in the day and mixed pies at night. Her pies tasted so good Gorman's Market contracted her to stock his two stores. While Miss Lucy mixed the pies in the aluminum pans, Frank Gorman packed them in his big store freezer. As fast as she mixed them pies, they were gone. She even had pre-orders for parties, barbecues, and whatever social happening in the surrounding towns just from word of mouth. After a few years, it grew harder and harder for her to fill those pie orders. But she did.

Miss Lucy and I had never been what you would call close. Not like some of the relationships that grow between the children of the maid and the children of the people the maid worked for. You know those friendships that are never developed on equal footing; nevertheless, they grow because of that old way of thinking that still lingers here in the Deep South. The kind that causes us to help one another in times of need but will never be seen socializing at each other's homes having tea and such.

Yet, Miss Lucy and I had mutual respect for one another. Even growing up together, we never played as little girls play together, but we had our private times when we talked – girl to girl. One particular occurrence happened when I was thirteen. There was this particular dress I wanted for the Federated Girls Club dance. This dress spoke to me from a page in the Sears-Roebuck Spring/Summer catalog. A light blue chiffon with spaghetti straps and a beautiful satin belt with rhinestones on a cloth buckle. The skirt part gathered at the waist and had an elegant sparkle to it.

I imagined myself dancing like the girls on American Bandstand in my blue chiffon dress. I had just started to develop my womanly figure and noticed that the model was tall and shapely like I was back then. Oh, how I wanted that dress. Nevertheless, it cost more than I would dare ask my mama to spend. So I just dreamed. I had even turned down the edge of that page so periodic glimpses in between my chores would be easy to maneuver.

Now every woman knows that when you turn down a page in a book, you're either reading or dreaming. And I'm not one to read the Sears-Roebuck catalog. I had been looking at that dress on an instance when I was supposed to be dusting the porcelain figurines in Mrs. Jacobson's curio cabinet. Miss Lucy came upon me suddenly and asked what I was looking at. Although startled, I found myself blurting out how much I loved that dress and how well it would go with the Peau de Soie shoes on page *such and such*. I fumbled through the pages, showing her the entire ensemble - the earrings, and the necklace and the bracelet; even the gloves. She said while laughing, "Don't forget the hoop slip."

Well that afternoon, we sat on her living room floor and looked at every page in that catalog, discussing details of the items that we liked and the ones we didn't. We laughed at the way the boys posed in their cardigans and loafers. I dreamed of having a French styled bedroom with the canopy bed. Lucy had one already, so I imagined it to myself. There were things in that catalog that Lucy wished for, too. She stared at some of the pages longer than I did so I turned those pages slower - the mother and daughter dress-alike models; the girls in the cute pedal pushers and sleeveless cotton blouses laughing it up in the fake catalog soda shop. Both of us lingered longer on the pages that highlighted that year's wedding dresses.

We found that we were more alike than not. But that was one afternoon out of the thousands that we did something other than just say hello or wave or smile our greetings at each other. We both knew our place in this world, and we were content in it. Miss Lucy didn't try to enter my world, and I indeed wasn't readily welcomed in hers. Like when I thought I was making a little social progress, Mama would just recite, "Southern white folks don't care how close you get to them as long as you don't get too high. And the northern ones don't care how high you get as long as you don't get too close."

I grew tired of hearing it, but I heeded it. Before too long, I understood it.

I'll always remember the day before the Federated Girls Club dance. I came home from school distressed that I had to wear my sister's old hand-me-down party dress. Not only was it a cast-off, but it was also the ugliest beige dress I'd ever seen. The beige isn't what made it horrible, though. It was the lace that covered it. All over. It had no shape to it, and the 'no' sleeves made it look like a fancy potato sack. Even worst, I had no high heels.

"You have to wait until you're thirteen to wear high heels," Mama had said.

"But I am already 13!" I'd remarked knowing that I had to wait until Easter to get new church shoes even though I had been thirteen for a couple of months.

I had saved some of the money I'd earned working, but most of it went towards Christmas presents for my family. I had about twelve dollars to my name.

I thought about wearing a coat over the dress, but it was March, and winter coat weather was over. Besides, I couldn't wear my old coat to the dance. The sleeves had gotten way too short on me, thanks to my latest growth spurt. And I had *accidentally on purpose* wasted cooking oil on it. The coat had seen better days. Both my sisters, Sarah and Sadie, did their time with that coat before me. I think it had originated from an older cousin who probably passed it on with pleasure, too. Then it came to be my time. Mama had said, "That coat is expensive."

Sarah said, "Somebody got robbed." We had laughed.

Then Mama said, "Wear it or be cold."

What would you have done with those freezing morning temperatures walking to school? The first day I walked out in public in that gray herringbone coat with the black velvet collar, I promised myself that not another poor unsuspecting relative would ever be sentenced to wearing "the Chesterfield." That's what we called it. It had become infamous. It was left up to me to retire it. So I did.

I went to the bedroom I shared with my sisters. My head hung down; depressed that I had to wear that ugly beige dress with flat shoes. They tried to console me by telling me how lovely I'd look with my hair up in pin curls and Mama's pearl teardrop earrings. But I had made up in my mind that I would be a wallflower. No dancing, no eating; just sitting there in a corner in the dark until the dance let out. That's when I found the big package all wrapped in brown paper; laying there casually on the bed. We were anxious to open it but more eager to see who had sent it. On the front of the mysterious package, written in big black letters, Miss Edna Mae Bennett. No return address.

Sadie carefully untied the string that held the package. Then Sarah ripped away the paper in one quick slash. In it were my young girl dreams - the entire ensemble from the

Sears-Roebuck catalog – including the hoop slip. Mama said she didn't know who had sent it. But I think she knew. I knew.

Miss Lucy and I never spoke of that dress. I did tell her that I had a wonderful time at my first dance. That was my thank you. That's how she wanted it.

We'd see each other from time to time after college. Usually at a distance, but we would wave to one another. Miss Lucy was teaching school on her side of town, and I was teaching my kids on my side. What I knew about her life then was what I heard from my mother. "Miss Lucy just left for South America" or "Miss Lucy just returned from Africa."

Sometimes, I'd read a line or two about her on the Society Page of the Lambert Chronicle; about some charity, her family had sponsored. However, this I especially remember. I saw her in the supermarket years back.

"Hi, Miss Lucy," Cordially, I said as we approached the counter. Although it was the late seventies and Lambert and everywhere else were very much integrated, habit or common courtesy forced me to allow her to step ahead of me in line.

Miss Lucy smiled as though she was happy to see me. She took my hand in hers and gave it a tight squeeze. She kissed my cheek lightly, too. Well, I felt splinters of electricity run through my entire body. Now you'd think that if you were being shocked by some high voltage or current, you would snatch away as fast as you can. I didn't.

I felt this peaceful shock (if there is such a thing, that's peaceful); like I had been recharged. It was the strangest thing I'd ever encountered. Now that I think back, that was part of Miss Lucy's soul I felt.

Some folks in Lambert said Miss Lucy was a bit eccentric, but peculiar is a better word to describe her. She was too pretty for eccentric. Very popular with the menfolk, too and could get any man in town to do just about any chores for her – and for free. We could never understand why she never married. She had beauty, brains, and money.

Mama said Miss Lucy rarely had female visitors after she returned home from college. That didn't mean she didn't have any women friends. Just none that close. She still smiled and went on with life – traveling to other continents and sharing her worldly adventures at one of the many Lambert society gatherings.

After years of only waving in passing, we just happened to meet up in Lambert's Drugstore one night. I hadn't seen her for years, and both our mamas were old ladies by then. I think we were called old ladies by then, too. We were in our forties.

Besides, our mamas had been ailing with one of those seasonal flu bugs that crept in on us before full winter set in. We'd been attending to them – in separate houses, of course. Mama had long since quit working for the Jacobsons. My dad had died and left the house, and the car fully paid for. She had his retirement money coming in, and what that money didn't cover we did, so there was no need for her to be a maid anymore. Besides, she was too old to pull those long stairs and clean that big old house. I'd heard that after Mama stopped working, the Jacobson's hired a maid service to come in two or three times a week. Said she couldn't find anyone as good as Mama.

Through our reminiscing and catching up Miss Lucy asked if I was still teaching. (I was.) It's funny how time has a tendency to mellow you out. Over several cups of coffee and lemon pie, I found out that she had retired years earlier and was running the pie business from her home. With her daddy and Henry both gone, and not having a husband or children, I suspected that she was a bit lonesome in that house with just her ailing mama. You know how you can see lonely in some folk's eyes. So, when she asked me to help her with the mixing of those pies, I jumped at the chance to do a good deed and to get my hands on the recipe for that prize-winning pie.

Yes, we all have ulterior motives for the things we do, but some things we do just because it's the decent thing to do. I don't claim to be anything other than what I am – hard working and enterprising. So I did expect to get paid to help Miss Lucy with those pies. Though, deep inside of me, I just wanted to help her.

Christmas break made the offer more inviting. I had some extra time on my hands since the school was out for two weeks. My boys were grown and on their own doing whatever grown men do. My husband, Percy had retired. He was spending more and more time on the fishing pond when he wasn't working in his garage on somebody's car. His hobbies, he said. Well, a man needs hobbies to keep his mind off impure things.

Miss Lucy offered me twenty-five cents a pie. I thought how generous since those pies didn't cost but two dollars in Gorman's Supermarket. Yes, Gorman's was now a large chain of grocery stores, thanks in part to Miss Lucy's pies. Folks from all over the southeast had heard about those delicious pies, but they were sold exclusively at Gorman's and packaged by Miss Lucy herself. I started figuring in my head…if we make a thousand pies a week, that's two hundred and fifty dollars for me and… We were going to be rich.

At first light, I was dressed and ready to travel the few blocks to the Jacobson place. Miss Lucy didn't give me a specific time to report to work, but routine had me up early that Saturday morning. I teetered around my house a little, dusting things that didn't need dusting and checking my houseplants for dry brown leaves and beetles. Percy slept peacefully as I walked out the door. I didn't see a need to wake him. I left his grits simmering way down low on the stove. His eggs and sausage were left on a covered plate on the stove, too. I didn't worry about a fire since he would smell the coffee brewing and be up soon anyway to go fishing.

Seven thirty found me knocking at the back door of the Jacobson house. The back door is where I had always entered. As a child after school and on Saturday, I came through the back door and left out the back door. That's what I did that cold morning. After several minutes of alternating knocking and rubbing my hands together to warm up, I decided I'd go on in.

"Miss Lucy," I called. No answer. I walked through the corridor that led to the servants' quarters. What a familiar smell in the air. Nothing had changed in twenty-five years, but time.

"Miss Lucy." No answer. Slowly, I strolled through the room. The old Pfaff treadle sewing machine Mama had used to stitch clothes and linen showed wear on the front edge of the base but was otherwise shiny and clean. Her white cotton apron still hung on the clothes tree. The little table with the metal top stood in the middle of the room. Two slatted wood chairs pushed underneath. I imagined Daddy sitting there bending over old newspapers shining Mr. Jacobson's fancy shoes. Giving them a 'spit' shine.

"Miss Lucy." I followed my memory down the short hallway to the kitchen. It had been remodeled with new appliances and cabinets. The stairway on the backside of that kitchen had been removed and with the extra space. Miss Lucy had added more counters and cabinets and a big tall see-through freezer. Every dish and utensil rested in its proper place. I smelled a hint of Clorox bleach. I wasn't surprised to find it spotless either. That's how she was - neat, efficient, and careful with the smallest of details. I could see her standing there mixing lemon pies or a surgeon performing an appendectomy for that matter. It was just that pristine.

"Miss Lucy," I called again. I worried that Mrs. Jacobson had taken ill in the middle of the night and Miss Lucy had rushed her to the hospital. I walked through the rooms in the downstairs part of the house. The curtains still pulled together. I opened them to let the bright sunshine through the window before I headed up the stairs. It seemed too quiet.

"Miss Lucy." Something wasn't right. I felt it. I knocked on Miss Lucy's bedroom door. It was ajar. Through the sliver of light that came through her Venetian blinds, I noticed an empty bed.

"Miss Lucy!" I walked down the long hallway to Mrs. Jacobson's room. I remembered the wall of old portraits hanging conspicuously; their dark eyes following me as I strode little by little. The door stood half-open, but I couldn't quite see inside. The windows on the west side of the house entertained the cluster of tall Live Oaks and Southern Magnolia trees that obstructed the sunlight. I hadn't noticed until then that the house felt icy cold. I shivered, "Mrs. Jacobson." I pushed the light switch on.

"Mrs. Jacobson," I called out once more. I was a little bit surprised Miss Lucy had left her there all by herself. I figured she had gone to the store and would be back directly. That's what I wanted to think, so that's what my mind let me think, for a moment. Then my better sense took hold of me. I went closer to see Miss Lucy lying peacefully in her mama's bed.

Ordinarily, I guess I would have been horrified to see somebody who had committed suicide. Nevertheless, at that moment, for some strange reason, I almost understood. Almost.

I saw the suicide notes on the bed table beside the empty bottle of pills and whiskey. I found out later Miss Lucy's mama had passed away late the night before. An ambulance had taken Mrs. Jacobson to Lambert General Hospital where she'd had a massive heart attack. I figured Miss Lucy thought she had no more use in this world. Alone. No children. No husband. No other family to speak of.

One of those suicide notes had been written to me. No explanation of why Miss Lucy chose to do what she did. Just some detailed instructions on fancy stationery paper. As if she took her time and thought about it. Maybe she had this scenario already considered just in case. Maybe that's why the house was so cold. Just in case I didn't come early enough. I think she knew I would find her, though - sooner or later.

The other note addressed to her lawyer had a handwritten paper, "Codicil to the Last Will and Testament of Rachel Lucille Jacobson" attached to it; leaving her estate to me, Edna Mae Bennett. I cried. I prayed. I thought what a wasted life. Then I dialed the operator for the number to the Sheriff's office. I wondered, first of all, how someone could take her own life. Like you have no more hope. I figured my life might not be rosy today, but tomorrow will come. Second Corinthians 1 and 19 tells us plainly, *He has delivered us from such a deadly peril, and he will deliver us again. On Him, we have set our hope that he will continue to deliver us.* That's my hope that tomorrow may be a brighter day.

I wondered why Miss Lucy left all her worldly possessions to me. We hadn't been close friends. I cared about her. Can't say I didn't. She was a strange woman, though. I guess, through all the years she had known me - and my mama, we were like family. We had a history. Seen each other almost every day growing up through the good and the bad. Our mothers were friends, I reckon. The best they could be in the times. I used to hear them talking about women things and laughing together sometimes when they thought they were alone in the house. One had even comforted the other when a husband passed.

By the time the sheriff and his people came, Miss Lucy's skin color had begun to change. The coroner pronounced her dead, and they wheeled her away on that stretcher covered up tight with just a thin white sheet. I called Percy to come get me. I felt too nervous to drive home.

Well, that happened nearly ten years ago. I never did get possession of the Jacobson estate. Never thought I would either. When the Coroner and those folks from the Probate Court got wind of the Codicil, they started looking at me funny; talking investigation. Besides, no witness signed on that legal paper. I guess Miss Lucy knew I might have trouble that's why she left me with the recipe for that sweet lemon pie. I read her note and used the

23

good sense the Lord gave me to pay attention to her instructions. The first thing she said was, "Edna Mae, take this note and hide it. It has my lemon pie recipe and the combination to the wall safe."

The second thing she said, "Use the two hundred and sixty thousand dollars from the safe and make some money from my recipe." I thanked God for giving me the presence of mind to bring my knitting bag that day. I had figured, we'd have some downtime, and I could finish my quilt. That big bag and my pocketbook had just enough room for two-hundred and sixty-thousand dollars in cash.

That's my picture on those boxes you see in the grocery store freezer. They're sold all over the world. *Edna Mae's Lemon Pie*. Shish now! You can't tell anyone what I told you about Miss Lucy's pie.

The Truth about Michael and Jaylan

IN THE BEGINNING

Jaylan

You could say I saw heaven when I first laid eyes on Michael. It was already warm that March morning on Emory's campus. The dogwood trees were just starting to blossom. The birds were humming love songs. And there he was. Tall, handsome, and dressed like a million bucks. We were both running late for our LSATs. He asked me for the time. He'd run out that morning without his watch. I thought it was fate that we met. I had lost my watch earlier that week and had just found it. Stuck between the car seats. When we entered the classroom, there were only two seats left, and they were side by side. Call it destiny - kismet or whatever. It was as if we were supposed to meet.

Michael

Jaylan and I hit it off the first time we met. She had on this short blue fitting dress. Nice long pretty legs. Yeah! And she was nice, too. Sweet. I had a feeling we were going to be friends. I asked her out that same day. But of course, she said no. I respected that. She didn't know me. Jaylan was different from the other women on campus. I don't know what it was about her. But time was on my side. I knew sooner or later she would go out with me. And she did. Huh, I was a catch. So I didn't waste any more precious time. We did the dating thing. You know if

25

a woman is right for you. A few months in, I took her to meet my family. My Dad and Uncle Leon patted me on the back. They all loved Jaylan.

Jaylan

I did play a little hard to get with Michael. He was a *pretty boy*. You know the type. Women all over the place. I didn't need any drama. And I was careful not to get my heart broken. But he was persistent. He'd call every night just to see how I was doing. What got me was the single red carnation he placed on my windshield every morning. He had me. So I went out with him. Just coffee at first. Then dinner, a movie, or the theater; the park. Oh! Those romantic walks in the park. Michael and I became inseparable. The next step was to meet my family. After all, it had been fate.

THE PROPOSAL

Michael

The time came when I wanted to spend the rest of my life with Jaylan. I gave Jaylan my mother's diamond ring. It was bittersweet since I couldn't share the joy with her when Jaylan said yes. I believe my mom would have approved.

Jaylan

At the Sunday dinner table, I broke the news that I was engaged to marry Michael. Mama seemed happy.

She thought college was the perfect place to meet a husband. "You are both looking for the same things," she said. "Higher learning, financial security, careers." My sisters thought Michael was a good catch, too. We were happy that we could plan our first wedding together. I remember my dad looking up at me over his horned-rim glasses. But he said nothing. He said nothing at all. I returned to campus late that night. I called him as I had done every Sunday night since I'd left home. But he died that night. The heart attack that took him took a small part of me, too.

Michael

Super Bowl Sunday was the best time to let everybody know I was getting married. We were all over at Uncle Leon's. The whole family. The men were in the basement watching the game. Aunt Emma was upstairs with the rest of the family. Everyone was glad that I was getting married. They stopped watching the game long enough to congratulate me and all that. We celebrated my engagement and San Francisco 49ers winning the Super Bowl Championship, that night.

THE WEDDING

Michael

We were married the summer the O.J. trial was the talk of the day. In the heat of the Carolina sun, we spoke our vows openly and made promises to live happily ever after as Mr. and Mrs. James Michael Barrett.

Jaylan

I said - I love you Michael and I will honor and cherish you always. As we embark upon the privileges and joys of our holy marriage, I will look to you as head of our home. I will love you in sickness and in health, in poverty and in wealth, in sorrow and in joy, and I will be faithful to you by God's grace, as long as we both shall live.

Michael

And I said - Jaylan, I thank the Lord for the love that has bound our hearts together. I will love and cherish you always. As we enter into the privileges and joys of life's most holy relationship, I will look to Christ to guide me in all matters. I will love you always - in sickness and in health, in poverty and in wealth, in sorrow and in joy, and I will be faithful to you by God's grace, as long as we both shall live.

The Minister

I charge you both as husband and wife, to preserve sacredly the privacies of your own home, your marriage, and your heart. "What God has joined together let no man put asunder." Let no one presume to come between you, or to share the joys or sorrows that belong to you two alone.

Michael

In an instant, we were husband and wife.

Jaylan

Mr., and Mrs....

YEARS LATER

Jaylan

I had hurt for so long until the pain didn't matter anymore. The slow ache in my heart became a part of my existence, and I learned to thrive in the hope that the death angel would come and take me soon. I'd awaken every morning alone in a bed bought for two. My body yearned for the touch it had grown used to but snatched away by time and ill feeling. Michael slept in another room. Alone, too. But contentment seemed to be his truth, and he thrived on that. I imagine he felt I was content too. I had ceased to complain. He had almost convinced me that love was still there. Almost. But I didn't fall for that nudge. I had known love and what we had wasn't it. Oh, there were trace particles that seemed to enter during a rare touch when we passed in the hallway late at night, our loins calling out. But moments later when the sweaty flesh cooled, the specks evaporated, and we, again, went our separate ways.

There had been those times I'd thought if we had had children that would be enough to embrace the bond we made together years before. But that seemed like a "pulling at straws" explanation of why we were at this place far in between love and hate. And like a calliope, it played us from one extreme to another depending on the weather, the phase of the moon, and our late-night walk.

I'd heard some say that true love doesn't fade or die but it goes through a metamorphosis; changing its shape, its color, its smell. If that is true, what color makes it okay to live in life's loneliest passageway and what form does love takes on when it ceases to fulfill; if it had no more smell. If someone watched us from afar, would he see nothing but specks, trace particles of what use to be love? An empty vessel longing to be filled!

A towering brick wall surrounded Michael and me. There was no clear way of escape without the bricks caving in on us. And if I were assured that the bricks would not just maim me but kill me, I would have long ago broken through. Many times, I'd thought of fleeing, not looking back. But I had nowhere to run. No clear path leads from hell.

Michael

Jaylan was always sad. I tried to make her happy. I gave all I had in me. We were not material people, so our lifestyle was modest in that sense. That's the way we wanted it. I guess. Anyway, she never complained about it. The house, I mean. She kept it clean. It seems that's all she did was clean and move furniture around, the sofa from one wall to another. Rearranging the cabinets and the drawers where I couldn't find a damn thing. I never complained much though. It seemed my complaining made her sadder, so I quit complaining. Hell, I stopped saying anything.

Early on when we were trying to have children, she smiled. She even started working on a nursery using yellow bits and pieces, and she didn't care if it was a boy or a girl. I didn't care either as long as she smiled. When the babies didn't come, her smiles started coming less and less until soon, she stopped smiling altogether. Not everyone was meant to have children. I guess we were in that category; the childless couples. That didn't make us less.

I worked hard trying to give her my heart. After years of trying to love her, I just quit. Nothing pleases a roving soul. See, Jaylan lived in this dream world of impractical unsteadiness. She saw the two of us askew; way, way off from reality. Like I told her, life doesn't promise roses every day, and neither did I. What I promised I gave. Love, in sorrow as in joy. Love was never enough. I had nothing more to offer. So what else could I do but take that back?

WHEN WILL ARRIVED

Will

It was strange. After all these years. How could feelings that had long been dead, reanimate so strong? Maybe they weren't dead after all. Just lying dormant like a virus; waiting to take hold again. I didn't mean for it to happen. A few phone calls. Emails. That's all it was at first.

It was nice. Asking me how my day was going and listening to me. Those early morning messages were stimulating like a freshly brewed cup of Maxwell House coffee. It became nourishment for me, and I began to look forward to this daily recharge.

It started so innocently. Just talking about the stuff that had gone on in our lives when we were young: teenagers; reminiscing about the past when we were in love and wondering why we didn't make it last; then realizing that we had different life plans. Still, it made me smile again, and I longed for this. I could sense the loneliness was there, too. That's probably why we let this happen. How could two people who are married to two other people make each other feel the way we made each other feel? I didn't feel guilty about giving the loved I'd promised to another. I didn't even think of my wife. I was sure what we were doing wasn't sanctioned by God or by man, but I felt invigorated by this affair, and that had made it right. It was fate. We were supposed to be together. That's what I thought. Then.

In retrospect, I should have known that our loneliness wasn't the same. I needed the warmth and not just a warm body. Then I'd listened to this televangelist one morning before our talk, and he said no man could get into heaven with a lover and a wife. Yeah, I was sure I wasn't going to get to heaven. And I was doubly sure I was going to hell because we'd both used each other; even though I'd said I was in love to make what I did seem less sinful. Then the email came. The early morning email with the subject line that always read, "GOOD MORNING" in big letters had changed. This new subject would be permanently etched in my head. The "LET'S BE GOOD FRIENDS" email that in essence said that we were both married, and we couldn't give each other what we'd like to. Huh, I wasn't angry about this email, I was mad at myself for not sending it first.

TOUCHÉ

Jaylan

Will made me realize that leaving Michael wasn't hard at all. What was hard was realizing I'd wasted ten precious years on him. Maybe the love that had started out wasn't love after all, but the idea of love. Come to think of it, ours was never the hot pulsating love that kept me thinking about Michael long after the loving was over. I came to terms with the fact that our marriage had been a showcase for family and friends who'd thought we made a "cute couple" since we were both so "cute." Two attorneys working for two of the most prestigious law firms in the city. By certain standards, we were the perfect couple. We hosted the perfect parties and cookouts a few times a year. They said we served the best margaritas in town. I question now if those mixed drinks mattered as much as the fundamental cleverness of our make-believe world. Michael's and mine. If we could pull off such a charade as this thing we called marriage, then mixed drinks and everything else we did was effortless.

Why wasn't I happy in a marriage with a man as good a catch as Michael Barrett? He had grown good-looking to the point of beautiful. Well-dressed, well-educated, great career. I was the envy of all my friends. Not bragging, but none of them had what I had, and I didn't even want it. Between the two of us, we earned exceptionally high incomes, but money is not a conduit for happy when there is no emotional paradigm.

Michael

Jaylan had felt responsible for the lack of potency in our marriage. She thought that what was wrong in the marriage had a lot to do with her and I guess she wondered if she had given all she could. Sure, marriage can go bland over time. There are things that can be done to revitalize ailing love, though. But what if the love is terminal? At first, she was angry with herself. Could she have been more open to how she felt about what was missing? Maybe she could have tried a little harder to be in love with me. A good example is when I made partner she couldn't have been less impressed. Sure, she gave me congrats and all that. She even threw a great party. A formal, black-tie kind of event, just the way I liked. Invited all the people who needed to be there. She wore the right dress and hired the right caterer. Everything was perfect. Well, almost perfect. All that was missing was her smile. Ah, but that's beside the point, now.

Jaylan

The time finally came when I wasn't angry anymore. Not with Michael; not even with myself. I suddenly realized that what was wrong between us wasn't me. No matter what I'd given to the marriage, it would not have mattered. The end results would have been the same. Plain and simple, Michael was gay. What an oxymoronic statement. Like being told your husband is gay could be plain and simple. But it was. What had happened between Michael and Will couldn't unhappen. Regardless of how much I tried to unwind the tape in my head when he told me, the replay was always going to be the same. He had admitted it plain and simple, "I'm GAY!" I think I felt relief when he told me, though. In a roundabout way, I was glad. It gave explanation of why my heart was in such disorder. Call it woman's intuition or God's intervention; we could never go back to that convenient place where we existed before Will.

Michael

Sure, Will had awakened stirrings in me that I thought I had suppressed forever. Despite how much you try to run from it, it's always there, right behind you; ready to pounce on you like a Bengal tiger. The only thing you can do is turn around and face it. I'm grateful to Will because sooner or later if it hadn't been him, it would have been someone else like him. After years of trying to go against what was naturally inside of me, I'm finally free. Jaylan has forgiven me. As best she can. Now we can both go on and try to find whatever happiness we can in this life.

Jaylan

If I'd really, I mean, really opened my eyes wide enough, I could have seen the real Michael years ago. There were those little hints that I jiffed off as Michael's quirky brilliance. Even his finicky ways and the incessant details of what to wear – for both of us – I'd conceded that I'd just married a Type A. Huh! Type Gay! But, I won't go back there now. All I can do is look ahead. The shroud has been lifted, and I see that there is a clear escape from hell after all.

Michael

Jaylan divorced me. She was kind enough not to bring our private life to the public. She's always been sweet like that. We split everything in half and those things that couldn't be split up, we played poker for them. Funny, huh? I still say she cheated in Five Card Draw to get the Table Rock property. But that's okay; she seemed to enjoy the mountains more than I did. The funnier thing is... she's my best friend now. All those years I tried to please her. Tried to be somebody I wasn't just for her. Lying to myself. Hell, I was lying to everyone. And all she needed was honesty. We're both happier now. That's the truth about Jaylan and me.

When Love Happens

Mr. Wallace and I were married for forty-three years when I woke up one morning just plain out of love. For some reason, I stopped liking the way he smelled. He didn't have any kind of bad odor, just old and boring. When I told him how I felt, trying to make things in our home a little bit livelier, all he said was, "Okay, Hazel."

That's the way he was - smooth flowing and easy, like the summer breeze. Not making a fuss; just going along with the program. But he could be a tornado when he had to be. I found it's easy to pick up and leave, too. Especially if you're determined. I was determined to live the last days of my life with some vigor and excitement. Mr. Wallace and I were both seventy-three. When we retired, I had hoped to travel, have some enjoyment out of life. But I guess that was my plan, and not his. So I left.

I only took what few things I needed to get set up in the apartment over my son's garage. I had made up my mind to make my new home in Macon, Georgia. I was living a full state away from Mr. Wallace. And I wasn't sorry for leaving him back in South Carolina, either My son and his wife seemed to like me being there with them. When they went to work, I worked, too. Cleaning that big old two-story house and cooking dinner every day. Making sure I fed them good. Lord knows my daughter-in-law cooked as if we all were on a diet like her. But I didn't mind it. It kept me busy.

I joined some senior groups, women's clubs, and got involved in the community of the living instead of being bored with Mr. Wallace. I went on some senior citizens' cruises and casino trips to gamble – spending what little money I had saved up. I took on a few babysitting jobs, too until those contrary children got on my last nerve. Children are different these days. Smarter, it seems, than when mine come up. Nevertheless, no money in the world would be enough for me to keep these children of today, again. Thank God, my grandkids are old enough to take care of themselves and go about their business.

After almost six months of club meetings and road trips, I found myself getting bored with those old people, too. You see I didn't like the way they smelled either. Like *Bengay* rubbing ointment. I started thinking more and more about Mr. Wallace, but he didn't seem to be thinking about me. He rarely called me to see how I was getting along without him. Although I had checked on him several times over the course of the few months after I left. He would tell me he was getting along okay, never offering anything else in the way of conversation. "Okay, Hazel." That's all he would say, "Okay, Hazel."

The time came for our granddaughter's graduation. Finally, I was going to see how Mr. Wallace was actually getting along. I was going to see if he was, in fact, *okay*. Well, the anticipated day arrived. My son had made all sorts of cookout plans. Had me basting meat, making potato salad, coleslaw, macaroni, and cheese, etc., etc. Now I'm thinking to myself aloud. "What y'all gon do?"

Anyway, I had stayed up all night cleaning chitlins because that what Mr. Wallace liked. You know you have to clean them things good, even when the label says pre-cleaned. Get all that stuff out of em, too. Then I had to rush upstairs and take my shower. Get dressed. You know. Look foxy. Now at my age, I wasn't looking too shabby. Not too much gray and I had lost a good bit of weight since I stopped cooking meat and gravy every day at my daughter-in-law's insistence. I reckon I was still attractive because I was still being asked out. I had dated a few old men, but that's precisely what they were. Old. Besides, they smelled dry and boring, too. Always wanting me to cook THEM some food. And I'm asking myself out loud, "What y'all gon cook for me?"

Mr. Wallace entered the room, and my heart skipped a beat or two. He looked the same as he did the day I left him, and wearing that same gray suit I bought him six years ago. It still fit him. He hadn't gained any weight. Why don't men gain weight as much as they eat? If a woman ate what a man ate, she'd be as big as a house.

Anyway, he still smelled dry, still looked dull and easy. But there was something different about him. On the other hand, was it about me? I went up to him and welcomed him in my special way. I know he was happy to see me since he specially greeted me with flowers; pink carnations. My favorite flowers. The whole time we were at the cookout, I hung close to him. You see, some old women there had eyes on my Mr. Wallace.

It's funny how love happens. Even with the person you used to be in love with. Something happens in trivial passing, and you find yourself back in love again. It could be the way he jiggles loose change in his pockets when he gets nervous; or fumbles with his ear while in deep thought. Or the way he hums when he's happy. The same things that made you fall out of love are seen in a different light; through different eyes; through different tears. What used to be never-ending bickering over small matters turns into caring and consideration; nagging is now cute.

You think all the heat is gone and you pass on to another somebody only to find that the other somebody can offer no more than the first somebody, with less passion, and less years. The same qualities that you loved about that person are still there, underneath the time, underneath the wrinkles and graying hair. And if you step back and look at yourself, you'll see that you haven't changed from that person in the old mirror, either. The same heart beats underneath that old shell.

I've been living in this world a lot of years, and I can say I don't know much about a lot of things. But what I know, I know. And what I know is that love happens. And there is nothing you can do about it. You can't make anybody love you. Love is like the weather. You can't control it. You just have to wait for it to pass and hope it doesn't do you any harm. It can be sunny one day and a terrible tornado the next, taking everything that's alive and healthy and making it weak and sorry. On those sunny days, it can be good, but we know the sun doesn't show up every day without some clouds. All you can do is hope the clouds hurry up and pass, so you can enjoy what little bit of the sunshine you get.

I went back home to Mr. Wallace a few days after our granddaughter's graduation. He didn't ask me to come back; I went back because I missed him. He was lonely for me too, even though he'd never say it. All he said when I told him I was coming home was, "Okay, Hazel." However, his eyes lit up brighter than I'd ever seen them. He came and picked me up, and I happily moved back to the same things I had left behind.

Mr. Wallace never did say, *Welcome back home, Hazel.* But he put all my belongings back where they were and asked me what's for dinner. I'm here to tell you, no matter what anyone says, I'm here to tell you from experience that when love happens, there's nothing to do but let it.

The Inheritance

Young Myra Jones lived with a sickness. Not from the usual illnesses that come with just everyday living. Her ailing started from that old virus called lonely. It hadn't snuck up on her either. Her lonesome was the kind you're born with and heaped upon you through inheritance. And like most birthrights, she hadn't earned hers. No matter what she did to quench that desperate hunger for closeness, it came hopeless. The burning in her soul for someone meaningful to hold and to hold her seemed endless. Even sweet words sometimes were enough to calm the storm raging inside her. Silent tears plagued young Myra, and she became the wall she'd long feared would engulf her.

Oh, there had been companionship of sorts; the boy who loved her for a few months then up and left her when it was no longer convenient. Wesley Newman had married the plain girl at the other end of the street who had less experience with *life* than Myra. He had come back once or twice, and Myra let him back in too quickly. He stopped suddenly when his conscience woke him up, and then denied ever knowing her. Before that, Richard Fleming, the young man from next door had satisfied her behind the shed room and later bragged about it. She could handle that. He loved *quick*. Not long enough to sauté and get into her blood. Those were just two on a list of ungrateful males who had loved her just long enough to burn. When the fire died out, the ashes turned cold and blew away, Myra was again left with only her inheritance.

By the time she turned sixteen, Myra had had more than her share of moments behind the shed. And almost everyone knew it even though they never talked about it, except behind closed doors – mothers warning their sons about the likes of her. Young and old boys telling other boys sordid details of things that did happen with her and of things that didn't.

All the same, Myra lived in a respectable house on respectable Normandy Street – the *right* side of town with Deacon Hezekiah Bentley. He was senile now from a stroke in the brain, and there was no need to talk to him about it. Mrs. Bentley died knowing that she was going to hell for not talking about it. Everyone just smiled and pretended that the sun that shined brightly on Normandy Street meant all was well.

How she came to be with the Deacon and Mrs. Bentley was a shame in itself. Myra was seven when the state took her in. Wards of the court. "Termination of Parental Rights" was on the court paper. The terms abuse and neglect were thrown around in court, too. Was it neglect? "The mother's out on one of her drunks!" a social worker had said when a concerned neighbor lady called again.

Mother did that often as Myra got old enough to fix cereal in dirty bowls since she was too short to reach the kitchen faucet. And even when she thought to pull up one of the raggedy kitchen chairs, there was no detergent. So the bowls were rinsed in cold water leaving with them the dried cereal from the night before. Sometimes there was no milk or spoiled milk, and Myra learned that corn flake cereal with a little water was palatable.

The Family Court Judge had said *yes* to the order then snatched them away from Mother and away from each other. The small ones – one, two, and three-year-olds – were taken quickly by people who thought they were salvageable. Myra's eight-year-old brother, who had already been diagnosed ADHD – *Attention Deficit Disorder with Hyperactivity* – was shuffled off to the Hamilton Home for Children where he got as much attention as he could until his eighteenth birthday. The last Myra heard, he had joined up with the Job Corp and moved to Tennessee. She never saw any of them again.

Myra had been placed in one foster after another until they totaled six, each one successively worse than the one before. Deacon and Mrs. Bentley were well into their fifties when Myra came to live with them. Nine years old by then, bright, and matured by life's unfortunate circumstances, she was painfully aware that the life the Bentleys lead on the outside was rosier than the one she witnessed the first night inside the brick house on the tree-lined street. At the foster homes, no one pretended to care. Most homes had more children than caring could embrace anyway, so Myra never expected anything other than what she received – food and a place to sleep. And that wasn't always eagerly offered.

She had preferred Mother. The late nights when Mother came home intoxicated from cheap whiskey, too tired to undress, she'd fall out spread eagle atop the bed covers. Myra would crawl beside her, cuddling close for warmth and comfort. The next morning when Mother sat crying in front of the faded mirror from lonely, Myra would brush Mother's long dark hair and be happy. Mother would hug her close to her bosom without any promises. Even then, Myra understood her inheritance.

At the Bentleys' house with her very own room lined with dolls, toys, and fresh paint, Myra had cried that first night for Mother's warmth. Instead, she had received Deacon Bentley's warm breath hovering over her face. In the darkness, she could smell the Ivory soap, but it was a stench to her. He'd climbed into her bed rubbing his old body against hers. She felt him press close against her and

46

she screamed. He didn't stop. She screamed again. He hit her hard across the face with the back of his hand. "Shut up!" he'd said in a low voice, but the tone was forceful enough for her to know he meant it. And he'd hit her again.

As he mounted her small body, she cried. Not from the painful aches pulsating from her face and between her young legs, she cried for Mother.

When morning came, Deacon Bentley smiled and stretched at his kitchen table. He said, "What a great morning." Not looking up from his morning newspaper, he discussed the day's events as if last night was an imagined event only in Myra's young head.

Mrs. Bentley poured the coffee as she'd done every morning for forty years. She'd cooked the watery grits and the bacon crisp just the way Deacon Bentley liked it. The eggs were over easy, and all served on fine bone china.

"Good morning, Myra," Mrs. Bentley said as the young child walked into the kitchen, the blood smeared nightgown's strap loosely hanging from her shoulder. "How was your first night with us, dear?"

Myra never answered that question. *How could she not know how my first night was,* young Myra thought. Her unnoticed tears ceased from falling down sad cheeks, and she left the room amid Mrs. Bentley's cheerful humming that carried a cheerless undertone. She experienced more nights like that first night though she learned to blank out that part of her life; occupying her mind with television or any fixation that kept her away from what was real.

Deacon Bentley was cruel, that was the reality. Mrs. Bentley's cheerful manner was not. That helped Myra cope. If Mrs. Bentley can smile on the outside even though she hurt like a wounded pig on the inside, Myra thought she could too. So she didn't fault Mrs. Bentley for not hearing her screams. In her young wise mind, Mrs. Bentley was being raped by him, too.

The other reality had come to her. She couldn't go to another foster home, anyway. Mother couldn't find her if she left; if they took her away. Mother had come looking for Myra before. That's why they moved her. Myra couldn't tell anyone about Deacon Bentley and his nasty ways. She made up her mind that she would endure all so Mother could find her this time.

Mrs. Bentley fell ill and was confined to her bed. Her heart had grown weak. Myra figured Mrs. Bentley would do anything to get away from him. Even die. She lay in bed still joyful, singing *Swing Low Sweet Chariot* wishing for the Master to come carry her home. Young Myra grew content, too. Not content that Mrs. Bentley was so sick, but satisfied that she needed around the clock nursing care. No longer would Myra suffer Deacon Bentley's night intrusions. *With someone else in the house, I'll scream. I'll cry louder and louder until someone come to set me free,* she thought.

When Mrs. Bentley died, Deacon Bentley started all over again. By this time Myra had made friends with whom she could spend nights away from Deacon Bentley, and who could spend nights with her. Those times had saved her, but there were those nights in between the sleepovers and her period that Myra wasn't safe. As she grew older, however, she resisted him. Bentley was growing older, too and there were fewer late-night calls.

In spite of her inheritance, Myra kept her grades up with the promise of college and one day finding Mother. And at seventeen Myra was finally free. One night when the moon was full, and the light shone brightly; Deacon Bentley had entered her room with the same arrogance as that very first night. But this night, she had had enough; she resisted. "No More," she had screamed. "No More! No More!"

After years of late night calls, he stopped because Myra had insisted – forcefully – with a cast iron skillet to his head. Hidden behind her bed lay the same skillet Mrs. Bentley had used to fry his bacon and eggs. This night, Myra used it for protection. She thought she had killed him when he fell. Myra nudged him with her bare foot. He managed to get up and stagger from her bedroom as blood dripped from his head down his half-naked body. He was never the same after that night, and there was no more abuse at early morning before the cock crowed on Normandy Street.

"Morning, Myra," the mail carrier said while giving her the stack of mail wrapped neatly inside a sales flyer.

"Good morning, Mr. Lewis," she said politely smiling. "It's a beautiful day, isn't it?"

He nodded and continued delivering the day's greetings on his blue-eagled bicycle down Normandy Street.

Myra cautiously peered through the bills, letters, and postcards, and other mail not addressed to her, until she found one that was. Tears rolled down her face, and she savored the salty flavor, laughing loudly and passionately. Myra impatiently ripped open the letter addressed to her. It was from Mother.

The Arrangement

My mama and daddy had been married about twenty years before he died. A virile young man in his thirties, I guess that was all the time he had for this world. My daddy hated coloreds. He said they were a waste of God's fresh air. For my part, I didn't understand why he said what he said. He was always trampling down to Bell Norris' house; the colored woman that lived about a mile down the road from us. Mama would say, "Ya daddy's going to get a taste of corn whiskey. He'll be back soon and take you boys fishin'."

I was twelve then, but, I'm figuring he was tasting more than corn whiskey. He always came back smiling and a little more sober than he went. That and the fact that Bell's boy, Ellis looked exactly like my brother Jedidiah. Except Ellis' blonde hair was curly and matted down on his head. Other folks in our small town knew it too and whispered about it. Both the coloreds and the white people. Bell's husband, Moyd was mostly away from home working or trying to find work. But he had to know it because he was darker than tar and every bit as shiny. Miss Bell wasn't no light woman neither. I know Moyd was mad about it. Every time he passed our house going to town in his old pickup truck, he'd look over at us mean like, and spit. Daddy would cuss and growl under his breath, "Nigger."

Bell Norris' wasn't the only house he went to, neither. Mama just held her head down and shut her eyes as if she was praying. Mama never said a thing to my daddy about his late night crawling. I could tell in her sad blue eyes she wanted to. But Mama was a Christian lady of modest means. You could tell she had been a beautiful young woman before my daddy got a hold of her. She had those long piano fingers. And talented too. Mama played the organ every other Sunday morning at Shaw's Pond Baptist Church when we had Sunday meeting. Old Reverend Milton Mallishaw shared preaching between our church and another Baptist Church in Great Falls. On the fifth Sundays, Reverend Mallishaw rested so nobody heard no preaching in neither church. Even though my daddy never went to anyone's church, he had said, "It seems to me that between two southern towns full up with Southern Baptists, you could find more'n one preacher to do the Lord's business more'n twice a month." Still, every other church Sunday, my mama sat poised in front of that dusty old Skinner pipe organ that was every bit holier than anything else I ever heard my whole life, singing *Shall We Gather at the River.*

My Daddy was named after his daddy, James Edward Lollis. I was a third. They called him Jimmy, Jr. Back then, I was Lil' Jimmy. Daddy was a good man when he wasn't drinking and shooting his mouth off, which was rare. But for me and my brother and our old beagle dogs, Bullet and Sweet, we had some fun hunting squirrels, rabbits, and coons with him. Every chance we got, from early in the morning until pitch-black night, we'd be out there in the woods drinking watered down shine and killing us a mess of them old varmints. Enough for three or four nights of suppers. Mama would say, "Hope y'all gonna clean em."

We'd skin what we killed and prepared the meat for Mama. She'd cook it just the way my Daddy liked them; deep fried in battered cornmeal. Sometimes she'd bake raccoon, and we'd have some stewed okra and tomatoes on the side.

One cold winter January morning when it was the fifth Sunday, and no church was in progress, we all went out to the woods to hunt. We packed up the dogs and our equipment in the back of the pickup, along with some dried meat and sugar water for snacking. That day, me and

Jed had asked Mama to come with us. All her cleaning was already done. She'd just be sitting around the house waiting for us to return late that night. Daddy didn't like it. He said Mama would get bored and wanna go home before we were done. But he said okay, anyway because we'd begged.

It was a little better'n noon when me and Jed were in the mood for some rabbit. Mama said we could go on our own, so we went west down by Morgan's Pond with our birdshot. We'd been there for an hour or two, and no rabbits were in sight. Unexpectedly, we heard shots and screams. They were coming from the direction we had left. Jed froze up because the scream sounded like Mama. I jerked him by the arm, "Come on. Let's go."

Frightened, he held tight to my hand while I led the way to see what that scream was about. We followed the trail towards where we heard the sounds; cautious since shots had accompanied the scream. Moving slow and ducking low, we soon got to a clearing where we saw Mama kneeling on the ground. My Daddy lay next to her motionless. We ran closer. I thought, maybe the gun went off and knocked Daddy down. That thought quickly left my head when I saw his upper body riddled with holes, blood seeping through. *Birdshot don't kill?* I had been shot a time or two with a BB gun - in the leg. *Birdshot aint the same as that?*

Jed yelled, "Daddy, Daddy."

Daddy still didn't move. I came closer. Mama clutched the rifle that was still warm. I fell down beside her and hugged her body that was still shaking from the cold and the recent event. Jed cried out when we saw the thick blood ooze from my daddy's head.

Daddy was gone! Just that quick. The air turned really cold, and I cried, too. Me and Jed hugged Mama real tight that day on the ground next to my daddy. One parent was gone. I guess we had to hold onto Mama for reassurance that she wouldn't leave us too.

Folks from all over came to pay their last respects to my family and to console my mama. Some thought about how sad she must be feeling for shooting her husband in a hunting accident. Others whispered other things that Mama overheard but ignored. Either way, we had company coming up that long dirt driveway to the house until the day we put my poor daddy in the ground.

Reverend Mallishaw told my mama that he couldn't give the eulogy at the funeral because he didn't know my daddy that well. He said "Jimmy wasn't a Christian man, Sister Lisabeth. He hardly ever attended church service. What would I say about him."

My mama gave him a long written list of nice things to say about Daddy. And if he didn't, she'd be playing the organ next Sunday at the Lutheran Church up the road. Mama said, "They've been after us for a while, now. We may have to go see what the preacher's talking about."

He just grinned and twirled his gray whiskers, "Sister Lizbeth that sounds like blackmail to me."

Reverend Mallishaw preached an electrifying funeral for my daddy. Folks talked about it weeks after. Not too many people knew all those good things my mama wrote about my daddy. I had to admit I didn't either.

On a chilly evening around dusk, me and Jed chopped and stacked firewood on the side of the house. My daddy had been cold in his grave for a month or so when Moyd Norris pulled up in our yard in his old pickup truck. He would have never come close to our house if my daddy was alive, I thought. I ran inside where my mama was cooking supper. I was the man of the house, and it was my duty to protect us. "That old nigger had better get off my property," I said with too much importance in my voice.

Mama reacted in a way I'd never heard seen before, "GIT BACK TO YOUR CHORES AND DON'T NEVER LET THAT WORD COME OUT YO MOUTH EVER AGAIN! YOU HEAR?" She yelled loud and boisterous, like that woman who sold bootleg whiskey down the road. Nevertheless, I complied.

From the kitchen window, I saw Mama pull a rifle from underneath her long apron. She had been clutching that same gun the day my daddy was shot. She looked around to see if anyone was watching her, then she handed it over to Moyd. In return, he pushed another rifle through the window of his truck into my Mama's hand. She slipped that one under her apron and tucked it right tight. The two of them talked for a few seconds. I saw Mama shake his hand before he slowly drove away.

Soon after that, when Moyd passed by our house in that old truck, he didn't look at us so mean, and he didn't spit anymore, either. Sometimes he'd wave, and I would see Mama waving back. Years later, when I was a grown man and had little ones of my own, Mama told me the real story about my daddy and that sad day in the woods. It seems we weren't the only ones hunting coon and rabbit that day.

Mama said, "Moyd Norris and his boy Ellis was out in the woods hunting food to feed the family. They were hunting illegally on our land when Ellis accidentally shot your daddy in the head with a round of buckshot. With the backward thinking of folks in these parts, they woulda strung Moyd Norris up for murder - knowing the bad blood between 'em."

Ellis shot his real father. Our daddy, I thought.

"Your daddy was dead. Nothing could bring him back. It wouldn't have done any of us no good for somebody else to be hanged because of an accident," she said. "Moyd was a decent hard working colored man. He didn't deserve that fate no more than you or me."

Ma had exchanged the rifles with Ellis in the woods that day. She'd said to them, "Go home and don't tell a soul what happened."

Mama told the sheriff that she had accidentally shot my daddy trying to kill a squirrel. She was a Christian lady, and my daddy didn't have any life insurance to speak of, so they closed the file on the case.

It's been many years since Daddy went on to see the Lord, she still reminds folks of some kind things about my daddy, and Mama still plays the organ every other Sunday over at Shaw's Pond Baptist Church.

Shall we gather at the river,
Where bright angel feet have trod,
With its crystal tide forever
Flowing by the throne of God? Refrain:

Yes, we'll gather at the river,
The beautiful, the beautiful river;
Gather with the saints at the river
That flows by the throne of God.

On the margin of the river,
Washing up its silver spray,
We will talk and worship ever,
All the happy golden day.

Yes, we'll gather at the river,
The beautiful, the beautiful river;
Gather with the saints at the river
That flows by the throne of God.

I know it goes something like that.

Reflections in a Faded Mirror

Some folks said she was born on the wrong side of the tracks. However, the wrong side of the tracks is always the other side of the one you're on. To ask which side Viola was born on would be absurd. She was born on the tracks.

In 1938, Viola Johnson was born dirt poor in a small place called Dark Town. At least that's what displayed on the handwritten signpost pointing there. The residents had long before called it Boggy Creek - even before the dissolution of 'legal' slavery. She often wondered who had named the small settlement Dark Town, yet she understood the why. Not for of the color of its residents, but there bore a gloominess about it. A hopelessness that had shown on the faces of the people – young and old. Yet, the sullen dull desperation seemed to be tolerable since they owned it. No matter how unacceptable it appeared to those on the outside, Dark Town belonged to them. The swampy land, the tall leaning trees that looked sinister in winter when bare, the muddy red clay, the old general store where the people purchased everything from food to furniture, and the shotgun houses, all belonged to them - and God.

Dark Town residents lived a world apart from the other coloreds known obligingly as the New Negro. The ones who had strived hard to shed their costly nappy locks with straightening combs and straighteners. Those who had strived even harder to lighten their expensive skin with bleach and white blood, yet preserving their ancestor's strength, all while seeking to taste the crumbs from the bitter American pie. The cities north of the Mason-Dixon Line had lured them. Those who still attended to the needs of their white counterparts while clipping the roots tied to the injustices of their southern mothers and fathers. Looking back only in disdain.

As a little girl growing up in her dismal world, Viola watched all the bad and the good that happened when the hard labor of the young men and women outweighed its resulting economics. She witnessed firsthand how the bearers of this labor gave up, gave out, or gave in when the work and the struggling hadn't paid off fast enough. Those who could get out got out, and many never came back, except for funerals - theirs or their kinfolks', while the others wasted away in the muddy abyss. She witnessed the good side and bad side of love, and the burden finances or the lack thereof placed on it. How young love that always began happily hardly ever sustained its passion very long. Sometimes the children came too fast, or other people got inside one of them or both. And when love did appear to last, it was a hung-down-head kind of love that seemed to make the lovers old too soon. Nevertheless, sad love is still love, so it was worth being called love. Viola grew up knowing some kind of love, and she longed to experience it.

Viola had met many people while waiting on customers at Miss Melinda's - a shanty of a diner by day and juke joint by night. There were rooms for rent, too. A makeshift motel built from recycled boards and other second-hand bits and pieces, yet tidy and livable. Just off Route 25 near the Oconee Forest, Melinda, a distant cousin of Viola's, operated the only establishment for many miles where colored travelers due north and south could stop for food, rest, and conversation.

She had heard tales of the unpleasantness of the colored traveler. Stories of white commercial establishments along the long corridors of U.S. highways that treated them with disrespect all while accepting the authenticity of their green dollar bills. Some had told her stories of merchants' refusing to sell them food unless they bought gasoline, and then sell them food from back doors, where prices were elevated too high for what they had received. However, most colored travelers had learned to travel with their fried chicken and pound cake in shoeboxes. Others packed fried fish wrapped in brown paper bags with white bread and hot mustard. Melinda's offered an acceptable option.

Other young women who worked at Melinda's were more experienced with the night customers' habits. Viola worked the morning shift, serving breakfast and lunch to the locals and early travelers. Some of the men passing through the diner/juke joint/motel showed an interest in Viola. They had engaged in mild flirtations then soon be on their way until the next time - never thoughtful or interesting enough to get to know. Still, Viola caught sufficient attention from one unlikely traveler. Stanley Bradley, on his many drives from the north to Jacksonville, had told her about his 'good life' in Philadelphia. He spoke of his wife who had died a few years earlier from a brain stroke and his grown children, who he rarely saw. He bragged of his house on Adelaide Street with the porcelain bathroom and the linen towels and his job as an insurance man selling burial insurance policies up and down the east coast.

With each trip, he brought with him alluring stories of the social and financial advantages of northern living. Soon he bought Viola expensive gifts and trinkets that were sparse or nonexistent in Boggy Creek. With his sophisticated clothes and his *hand-me-down* charm, he methodically enticed Viola, all while spouting out words like love and how she would learn to love him - in time. It had been only six months, so Viola hadn't worried that she still didn't love him. She was young. She had time to learn, she thought.

"Hurry up, Viola." Stanley had called to her from the bottom step of the old wooden house. "We got about an hour to get on the road."

"I am. I mean, I'm coming, Stanley." Viola looked in the old faded mirror on the dresser at the fair-skinned woman staring back at her. She grinned at the fact that the mirror had distorted how she could almost pass if it were not for the broad nose her mama gave her. She grew tall and thin like her mama, too. That's what they had told her. She didn't know her mother and never would since she'd been dead most of Viola's life.

Walking out the front door in the heat of the March noonday sun, the gray wool suit, wearing warm on her skin, Viola tried to look older. She didn't. The high heel of her white wedding shoe wedged between the wood boards on the raggedy front porch. She grinned silly-like; embarrassed that she was clumsy on her wedding day.

"Come on now, girl. You walking kinda slow," Stanley said, straining while he picked up the wooden trunk that held all of Viola's life.

She thought how funny coming from a man almost three times her nineteen years. Nevertheless, Stanley had a prize to take back to Philadelphia. Something proud to show off. Viola was young, full of life, energy, and potential, and she was beautiful. He had found someone to validate his, albeit aging, manhood. Someone to care for him, to cook and to clean his house. A willing sacrifice.

On her wedding day, with all the well-wishers long gone, Viola's grandmother, Vinie, who had raised her since birth, tried to be satisfied. *She's married, now. She gon be all right.* But worry grabbed a hold onto Vinie and dug in deep like a burrowing worm. She forced a counterfeit smile. "Give yo granny a hug," she said while gumming down hard on an old black tobacco filled pipe.

Water filled her eyes. "Bye, Granny," Viola whispered.

"Don't say 'bye,' girl. You talking like I aint go see you no mo." Vinie propped up on her hard-dried sugar cane walking stick. She reached for Viola, the same way she had done when Viola was a little girl and had fallen down, or gotten stung by a mean wasp, with the love of a mother. "Just hug yo granny and git."

Stanley lugged Viola's belongings to his new yellow '57 Oldsmobile that idled on the muddy road. He had no notion to stay in those backwoods no longer than it took to pack up his bride. Then the massive trunk fell from his sweaty hands. PLUNK! He swore, "DAMMIT!" Muck from the rain-soaked red clay splattered on his sharp new suit. He yelled, "COME ON HERE NOW, GIRL! LOOK WHAT YO TRUNK DONE TO MY NEW CLOTHES!"

Vinie saw the anger that built up in Stanley. It had come too quick for her liking, and she feared for poor Viola. She'd seen anger like that before. Not anybody who could be happy as a lark singing in a tree one minute and stone cold mad like a rabid dog the next was good for sweet Viola.

Vinie had been witness to that same rage before, and she remembered:

They had come smiling wit dem yellow teeth showing; looking for my Uncle Minor. "We aint gon hurt him," they had told my papa. "We just wanna ask him a few questions." I was

64

a young girl then - not yet exposed to the cold reality of angry white people. The false smiles had quickly turned to stone cold meanness when Uncle Minor emerged from the shed. I saw them ripped the skin clean from my uncle's back with the same rope they used to hang him.

"That Stanley's got a mean streak just like dem," Vinie mumbled. "Be careful my child. I'm gon pray that the Lord's gon be with you." With her head down, Vinie waved goodbye to poor Viola.

The bittersweet memories of Vinie's children played in her head as she saw the last member of her family drive off. She had thirteen by birth, and then God saw fit and gave her Viola to ease some of her lonely.

Vinie's frail body led folks to wonder how she could have borne the thirteen children - the source of the love and the sorrow that rested heavy on her heart. She had told Viola:

> *Thirteen young'uns was the Lord's doing, not mine. We just did what the Lord say do. Go forth and multiply. Nine boys and four girls the Lord gave me and Eugene. Not a one of 'em sickly. I ax the Lord since he had done give me all these chirren, is he gon help me feed 'em? Lord said yes. And he did. We dun the best we could do. Then the Lord took some away. The County took some, too. The others dun forgot you and me.*

Some of the family, now buried in the Smyrna Baptist Church graveyard, dead from diseases, old age, and bad lovers. Some sat in an Aiken County prison for things other folks said they'd done, but with no admission from them. Others lived in other places - some known, other places unknown or forgotten. Some still visited when an occasion called for it like – Thanksgiving and Christmas when melancholy would set in. Nevertheless, rarely did they stay past the day. Some had even invited Vinie to leave Boggy Creek for a better way of living. She had just grinned and said she had family there to tend – meaning the family graves that she visited and cleaned regularly.

Viola's mama had left because of love. She returned to Dark Town, carrying with her, little Viola, and tuberculosis, to die in the state sanatorium. Not only from disease but of heartache for a man she loved but the social order of the day said she couldn't. Now Viola's turn came up to leave. Her departure proved bittersweet, too.

After her marriage to the elite Mr. Stanley, Viola entered a brand new world north of the Mason-Dixon Line. She had been able to move around without difficulty in both worlds - the world of the somewhat privileged and her cheerless Dark Town reality - unnoticed that she didn't fit in either. Although the people of her new association were obviously different from the ones she had been used to, Viola managed to blend in. Moreover, while her former world was filled with the harsh certainty of scarcity and inequity, she was comfortable with its legitimacy. Not that the new place was uncomfortable; she was uncomfortable with it. She found it difficult to understand how those who looked so much like the ones she'd left behind, could so blatantly deny them. The only difference she witnessed was luck. The new group thrived in it, while those in her old world didn't seem to know that it existed. Moreover, for her time with the elite, Viola hadn't imposed herself on them. Instead, they had exposed themselves to her. All their brute callousness disguised as privilege. Disguised as love.

Stanley provided Viola with the pleasures of life, but with a foul downside. New cars and fine clothes substituted for love came with swollen, black, and blue. Two tickets to Niagara Falls was the love he gave her for the baby that died inside of her because of a slow punch in the stomach when dinner was cold. Then there could be no more babies. The love in a shiny half-karat diamond ring could not be substituted for a broken leg from a hard push down some plush stairs. That love brought on a permanent limp. No matter how much love she could give, would never equal what Stanley gave her – swollen, black, blue, and broken.

On a dull February night when the Philadelphia air was frosty, Stanley lay bloody, cold, and still on icy steps. "He slipped and fell, officer," Viola announced as she cried crocodile tears through puffed-up eyes. "His head hit the corner edge of the brick steps."

She cradled her face in blood-stained hands. "I found Stanley there. Not moving. Not breathing. On the steps."

The outside steps witnessed something different, something more engaging than just a slip and fall. That night she had burned the rice. Fear gripped her as she tossed the rice out the back door.

Although elite, Stanley was still Negro, so "accidental death" was passable at the inquest. No more questions of Sweet Viola from family or friends. A 'wake' and a proper funeral was all they expected before life quickly returned to normal. When the buds of the dogwood trees opened their eyes, and spring drew near, Viola walked away from the elegant house on Adelaide Street where she had lived a life in slow motion for five long years. Neither the sophistication of the people nor the beautiful things had impressed her enough to remain. Running back to her old world of meagerness and simplicity was as natural as the constant mid-summer humidity that still overwhelmed Boggy Creek.

Love soon came for sweet Viola in a suitor worth the wait. She didn't have to learn to love. It burst forth natural and flowed smoothly like a southern evening breeze. No more would she see life as a just her reflection in a faded mirror.

The Love You Find Once in a Blue Moon

You might say I was a good cook. Big biscuits and thick sorghum for breakfast! Fatback, too! Meaty ham hocks swimming in a big pot of black-eyed peas for supper! Stewed chitlins and hog maws for New Years! With collard greens to bring good luck for money! Fried hoecakes to sop up the gravy! Apple fritters for my baby! Yeah! That was me, Darlene Baker. I had been cooking like this all my life. No wonder I got so big. A size twenty-four dress on a good day. Thirty-five years old, and my baby, Ernest still loved me. Told me so every time I fried some catfish and whiting! Cooked it about twice, three times a week. He liked my butter pound cake, too. And he never gained a pound. He'd say, "Doll? You know how much I love you, Baby?"

I'd answer him with a light kiss on the mouth, "More than air."

Ernest worked hard building things for people. He worked six days a week doing carpentry and laying bricks, so we could live a good life. He built the house we live in with his own two hands. It aint big and fancy, but it's cozy, and it's ours. Daddy gave us a piece of land next door to them. They thought we'd put a doublewide trailer on it. But we wanted a house. He built four large rooms and a nice big kitchen for me to cook and move around in. Custom cabinets, inlaid stove, and a great big island to prepare our meals. I remember, saying, "Paint it yellow, Ernest."

He asked me, "Why yellow, Doll?"

I said, "Ernest, my love, with a yellow kitchen, no matter how dreary it is outside, we will always have the sunshine in our home." Ernest laughed, and went out and bought the brightest yellow paint he could find.

The work was coming in steady for Ernest, too. He built garages for some folks in town for a reasonable rate. You know how it is. When a neighbor sees another neighbor with a nice garage, they will try to outdo it and build a two or three-car garage. Some of those garages were bigger than the homes next to them. Then somebody else would ride by and ask, "Did Ernest build so and so's garage?"

By the end of summer, Ernest had put up seven of the damn things. Jealousy is the green-eyed monster like they say, and we rode that beast all the way to the bank. Since our economic standing in the community had risen, Ernest told me to quit my job cashiering at Wal-Mart, so

I could be home when he was home. And I did. There is not a thing wrong with minding what a man tells you to do when he's good to you. And Ernest was real good to me.

Sunday dinner! I made potato salad! Macaroni with lots of cheese. The mustard greens were little bitter, though. Nothing a little brown sugar couldn't fix. Sweet iced tea and sweet cornbread. Melted butter on top. Fried chicken smothered in gravy. I didn't cook rice. Mama said, "That's too much starch."

Sitting at the kitchen table, just my baby and me. He was looking at me smiling, while he was eating. And I was looking at him and smiling, thinking about what he was going to give me that night, and the next morning, too. Ernest was a good man and the best at sweet loving. Out of the seven years, we had been married, he never let me down. I think that's why I was always smiling. I still remember the first time.

He had come over for dinner. I had made a juicy pot roast with red potatoes. I fixed a couple of nice smoked ham hocks in some fresh pole beans, some rice and gravy and cornbread. Oh boy, did he eat that up! His head only lifted up from the table to answer questions Mama and Daddy threw at him. And most of those responses were nods and grunts. Daddy asked, "Who your people, boy?"

"Sam Baker's son, Sir," Ernest answered with his head down. He was not disrespectful. His mouth was full. I laughed. It's nice looking at a man enjoying your cooking.

71

At the end of the meal, I served him hot peach cobbler and freshly churned ice cream for dessert. Afterward, he helped me wash the dishes. That was the first sign I knew Ernest was a good man. Although I had known him for years, we never had many conversations until he returned home from doing a stint in Iraq.

How we first got together? *One day, way back when, Ernest Baker strolled into Walmart, looking like a piece of smooth-running equipment in his army fatigues. He was what we southern girls call tall, dark, and a handful. As luck would have it, Ernest passed through my checkout line saying hello in a voice as smooth as ice cream. I laughed when I saw what he took out that big shopping cart. Boloney and white bread. I joked, "You not gonna get some cheese to go with that?"*

"Naw, I'm waiting for you to invite me over for dinner." The way those words fell from his lips, and the look he gave as he stared straight into my eyes, made my whole body quiver like a big bowl of Jell-O gelatin.

He came through my line a lot after that day. Always laughing and joking, asking me when I was going to invite him over for dinner. So this one day, before he could get the asking from his lips, I said, "A girl might want to go to a movie and get to know a man before she invites him over for dinner."

He followed that bold statement with, "Miss Darlene, how would you like to go out with me." I said yes, and the rest, as some put it, is history.

It took me a few weeks to invite him over for dinner, though. A woman needs to be sure what a man is up to before she starts offering up prizes. So later that night, after our bellies were full, and Mama and Daddy were in their room watching TV, me and Ernest spent time on the screened front porch, talking and snuggling and catching some of that cool crisp breeze that runs through Aiken County on a late September evening. As we fooled around a little bit on the porch swing, he got more acquainted than I expected. He had tried to put his hand up my skirt, looking for more dessert, I reckon.

"Stop, Ernest," I said halfway meaning it. I didn't let him go no further, though. Besides, if I had opened my legs wider for him to complete his investigation, I would have knocked him clean off the swing. After a while, he left with a few plates of leftovers from dinner. "I'll call you later, Darlene," he said. "I love you."

I-LOVE-YOU. There are no sweeter words in the English language. I thought about Ernest Baker until tired dragged me off to sleep. However, that wasn't the end of our night. Ernest came back.

He tapped lightly on my window. "Darlene," he whispered. "Let me come in."

Still half asleep, I opened the window. Ernest crawled in, knocking over the red ginger jar lamp…breaking it. "Shush," I said with my right index finger over his mouth. He moved my finger away, and

I replaced it with my lips. I was still spellbound from earlier that evening, thinking about his soft lips on my mouth and his sweet tongue thrusting in and out; his warm hands slowly moving up my thighs. The fall moon was full and bright that night and bound by a dark blue starless sky. His muscular body cast an unforgettable shadow as he stood in the moonlight. His eyes were nearly as bright as the moon and staring down. I fell back on the bed slowly, lifted up the comforter, and moved over just enough to let him lie next to me. He pulled me closer to his body that was warm like freshly baked biscuits. I heaved a quiet moan as he rolled over on me. Smooth and gentle, our love flowed free and easy until we saw the morning sun peeping through the trees outside my window. Yes, Ernest had finished what he started on my front porch swing earlier that night, and we've been together ever since.

I was late for my appointment that day. Didn't really want to go. Ernest said, "You ought to go, Baby. For me."

I went. The doctor said my pressure was up. Must have been the pig feet and cabbage I ate the night before! Sugar up a bit too! He shook his head, gave me some pills, and sent me on my way. I guess he thought he can control the disease but not the people with the disease.

I stewed some turkey wings that night. Cut back on the frying. Maybe use some smoked turkey instead of smoked jowls for my greens, like Mama. Ever since Daddy's heart attack last year, she'd been cooking differently; using recipes from *The Diabetic Cook Book*. Mama and Daddy must have lost over fifty pounds apiece. They didn't look like themselves. Me and Ernest stopped going over to their house for supper on Wednesday. She and Daddy stopped coming over to our place Sunday dinner, too.

We still shopped together, though. Mama drove to the Farmer's Market for fresh fruits and vegetables. They sold those sweet big red apples. She had bought some for her and Daddy to snack on. I thought about buying some to make a delicious apple pie. I purchased chow chow relish instead. We put a little on our collards since I decided to stop seasoning them with smoked ham hocks. See, Mama had had an influence on my cooking. Instead of frying all my chicken and fish in Crisco lard, I started using vegetable oil. I stopped cooking pig feet, too.

The night they pulled up to our driveway, the loud whining siren and red blinking lights scared the neighbor's dogs. They barked continuously until Ernest was strapped tightly to the stretcher and carried away. It was pitch black dark that night. I followed as close behind them as I could. I saw the bright lights of the "Emergency Room Entrance" sign getting closer to me, but I didn't remember the drive there. By the time I parked my car, they had already wheeled him in and hooked him up to every machine imaginable. His shirt was off. I remembered they had ripped it off at the house. One of them had pounded on Ernest's chest, while I cried. The other one placed something over his mouth that helped him breathe steadily. I was still crying when the doctor came to talk to me in the cold hospital waiting room.

It was hard to believe that Ernest had a heart attack! Everyone said he was in good shape. Not overweight, muscles everywhere because he worked all the time; hammering nails and lifting boards, and he was 'too young!' He had just turned thirty-seven the month before. We didn't see it coming!

"I'm so sorry, Ernest," I said while he was laying up in that hospital room, unable to speak, tubes running from all those apparatuses to his body. I could kick myself because all I could think to say to him was, "Sorry."

I waited in the hospital room with him day and night, praying to God through Jesus. *"O heavenly Father, who in Your wisdom knows what is best for my Ernest. Glory be to God. Lord, remove this sickness from him. Praise Your Holy name. I do love my Ernest, and you promised not to lay no more on me than I can bear. In the name of Your Only Son, Jesus Christ, my Lord, and Savior. Amen."*

Then the devil in me wouldn't let well enough be, and I selfishly added, *"Please make my Ernest whole again for me, Lord."*

God made my Ernest well enough to leave the hospital in less than three weeks. We moved over to

Mama's house to help us out. Although our household bills still needed to be paid, Ernest was recuperating, and I couldn't find steady work. Carpenters work on contract, so Ernest didn't have sick pay. Thank God, we had saved for a rainy day. And it seemed to be pouring. We had enough to pay health insurance to keep Ernest seeing the heart doctor. But money runs out when it aint being replaced. I wanted to find work. Went looking, too. Then I heard one of the cashiers at Wal-Mart said I was too fat to work. Maybe I was too fat. Yet, since we had been living with Mama and Daddy, I sure was losing some weight. Shucks! Mama cooked like everybody in the house was on Jenny Craig's diet. Serving lemon chicken and asparagus, pork tenderloin with seasoned vegetables and baked sweet potatoes, or roasted turkey breast and cauliflower for dinner. Lentil soup with saltines for lunch? It didn't taste bad, it just wasn't enough. That kind of food was good for my Ernest while he convalesced. Me, too. I guess.

Trying to get your Social Security benefits proved to be harder than we thought, like pulling hen's teeth; even though you worked hard all your life, paying your money on time because you don't have a choice. Uncle Sam sees to that. Ernest had worked since he was sixteen, served in the army, and then paid fifteen percent of what he earned as a self-employed contractor towards social security taxes. But what Social Security wouldn't pay Social Services did. We were not too proud going on welfare. You do what you have to do to survive. Ernest received a check for one hundred and seventy-nine dollars and two hundred and seventy-one dollars' worth of food on an EBT card. The money was just enough to pay the insurance on the truck and the EBT card saved us from being entirely dependent on Mama and Daddy. Although Mama said they wanted us there, four grown people living under one roof can tire each other out when not everybody's contributing.

It had been three months living with my folks. We had gotten adjusted to Mama's cooking, but Ernest didn't look too good. He had lost a good bit of weight he couldn't afford to lose. With my worrying and not cooking and eating like I wanted to, I lost thirty-five pounds. I didn't look too good, either. I did get that cashier job at Wal-Mart, though. Standing on my feet all day at that checkout counter took more weight off. Ernest said I looked good and tried to give me some good loving. Lord knows I was ready, but I didn't think he was. He said rubbing up beside me every night was gonna give him another heart attack, so I moved back out to the living room sofa. After about a week, I missed him, so I went back to the bedroom, and we made love like teenagers. It was better than before, like new love with old lovers, if there is such a thing. Ernest didn't have another heart attack, so we enjoyed each other the next night, too.

A year went by. Ernest had recovered well enough that the doctor gave him the go-ahead to start back to work full time. I thanked God that we were back at our house. We had a lot of work to do to get our place back in living order. Funny how a house is just like a person. When no one's there to give it tender loving care, it looks sad and lonely. Ernest gave it a new coat of paint, inside and out. I dusted everything thoroughly and cleaned with bleach and pine soap. I hung bright new curtains throughout the house. Made fancy new throw pillows for the living room sofa, too. I even made some changes in my kitchen. I got rid of the Crisco. See, I don't cook the foods that made my Ernest sick, anymore. Once the taste leaves your mouth, you're better off. We try to exercise regularly and eat healthier. I'm a size ten now. Ernest said he'd love me no matter what size I was.

Sometimes I worry about not cooking my old recipes for Ernest, but he seems to enjoy whatever I cook. Mama said a man aint too particular about the food as much as he is about who's preparing it. If a man loves you, your cooking is always gonna be good.

I baked a chicken last night. Seasoned it with some garlic and lemon pepper. Seasoned my fresh string beans from the Farmers Market with a little lemon pepper, too. I found out that brown rice cooked with love taste just like white rice and gravy. Made a banana pudding though. Can't give up everything. Sitting at the dinner table, Ernest reached over and squeezed my thigh, "Doll? You know how much I love you, Baby?"

I answered him with a light kiss on the mouth, "More than air."

Nobody's Friend

I met Franklin Hurst when I was 21 years old. He was twenty-three and married with children. I didn't know about either, at first. But that was my fault. Mama brought me up to recognize the signs. She said the signs are always there if you want to see them. When I look back, I did see them. Nevertheless, hindsight is still useless to a woman in love. Let me caution you though, my love story is not for the fainthearted.

The night I met Frankie, I was looking for love. Qualifications, not much. Just moderately tall, relatively handsome, and a reasonably good job. I was young, not realizing that the most essential qualifications didn't reside in the physical. If the truth be told, I was ready to get married. Living at home with twelve other people, it made sense to me to try to move on. Right?

It seemed my grandma didn't know how to say 'no' when folks needed a place to stay. So every relative on hard times took up residence at our home. As many as fifteen of us had squatted in that old dilapidated two-story house at one time or another. Growing up, it appeared huge. Five bedrooms, plus another small room off the kitchen. The wrap-around front porch with the hanging flower planters was nice and cozy. It could cause the most industrious person to find himself lazing around on the soft cushion of one of the grandma's wooden rocking chairs. The house was always filled with lively people – inside and out. Most of the neighborhood kids played in the front yard among yellow cornflowers and a spotty grass lawn. But we dared not set foot in grandma's living room; no one else either, for that matter. That room was off limits to everyone. Grandma said it was for company, but there was never any company because grandma treated everyone like family.

Since my mama never married, and never left home, even after I was born, our room was seemingly secure. On occasion, one of my 'uncles' would sleep over, leaving me to find other accommodations in the crowded house. That wasn't always ideal, especially when an 'uncle' who consumed a bit too much whiskey, forgot that I was Beverly's daughter. Many nights, I had to fight off one of her drunken sleepovers. Good thing, mama taught me how to protect myself from unwanted attention with a swift kick to the groin.

I guess Chanel and Janel's mother, my Aunt Sweetie, just forgot she had dropped her twin girls off for Gramma to babysit twelve years ago, too. Oh, she'd been back to visit. Even sent money every now and then. When they turned eighteen, I was sure they'd move somewhere else. But they are attached to that old house like bees to a beehive. Other aunts, uncles, cousins, and even neighbors in need have been in and out of Grandma's good graces. They would come live until they could "spell able" and then move on; some came and went many times over the years. Nevertheless, my grandma is no fool. If you're grown and able to work, you have to contribute to the house or, as she phrases it, "Get to stepping."

The South Carolina Department of Health and Human Services hired me full time after months on temporary part-time status. Even then, the job barely paid enough for a ride, health insurance, and clothes, let alone renting a place of my own. Still, I was determined to find a man, have two or three kids, buy a new and a house uptown somewhere, and be happy. That wasn't too much to ask for out of life. Or was it?

That night started out ruined. A flat tire on a Friday night wasn't the worse part. The spare tire was missing. Wasn't it supposed to be in the trunk when I bought the car from Dorian? That's the law. But when you pay $500 for a 15-year-old car, you're blessed if it starts up every day. I figured I was lucky with that much going right. In the two months since I had released my five crisp one hundred dollar bills to Dorian, I hadn't had one problem. Until that night! If that wasn't bad enough, I had just filled the gas tank that did me no good sitting up with a flat tire and no spare. Still, Friday night is party night. I couldn't let car troubles stop a party.

Dorian had the nerve to charge us - me, Chanel, and Janel - six dollars to drive us to the bony Room. "Damn straight, gas money," he chuckled as he snatched the dollars from our less-than-eager hands.

THE BONY ROOM, a favorite pseudo-swank nightclub uptown, catered to the up and coming "wanna-be-somebodies" in and around Lambert. The place started out as THE EBONY ROOM. When one section of the lights on the sign went out, the owner took his time replacing it. I guess he figured why he should spend good money when the bar was up for sale anyway. When the new owner took over, he didn't change it either, and it's been that way ever since. The missing light on the sign looked tacky - for a while. Most people will get used to just about any situation if it lasts long enough, as my story will soon reveal.

The crowd came dressed out in their high-end gear that probably cost them most of a paycheck. Some chatted with people on the other ends of iPhone 6s and Android 8s, while hooked up with others who were doing the same thing. No one had a conversation with who he or she came with, but then who was I to criticize? I melded right in with the rest of the socially unconscious of my Z generation.

Hanging out on the weekend proved to be a special occasion for us - Chanel, Janel, Dorian, and I. We looked forward to dressing up and escaping our dull weekday routines. We looked like new money, too. Our hairdos brand new, and face beat. I rocked a close and natural cut. Chanel and Janel preferred the braids and twists that made no sense seeing how their hair was just coming off of a ten-year perm binge. My mom said, "A different hairstyle never hurts as long as you take excellent care of it." We shall see.

Dorian's fresh color rinse exaggerated his natural curls that hung shoulder length. The dark blue blended well with his new eyeliner and melon blazer. My red spandex dress danced in the glow of the Coors Light neon sign that hung leisurely behind the bar. I just knew some nice-looking, well-intentioned "gentleman" would want to propose to, at least, one of us that night. Dorian said sarcastically, "Nobody's gonna ask y'all to dance. You look too desperate." Hindsight, again; I think we did seem a little desperate, and eager to please. In any case, I did.

We mingled with the people we knew, and the ones we didn't. The music was loud and boisterous. Even though I was a millennial, I hated *hip-hop* and *rap* with a passion. I patiently waited to hear some *Joe* and *John Legend*, which came sporadically in drips and drabs. Then it happened. Frankie, who had looked me up and down when I strutted in the club trying to appear mature, winked at me. He had sexy green eyes that seemed to radiate through me. The first sign. Mama had told me to be careful of men with sexy green eyes. No other explanation, just "be careful." Nevertheless, I didn't want to be careful. Careful was boring, and I was tired to death of boring.

My cousins and I strolled over to the bar stools that had just been vacated by some folks headed to the dance floor. We acted like five tons of special as we hopped in the seats. I crossed my legs and tried hard to pull my dress down, at least to my knees – enough to seduce, but not to satisfy. We all ordered Singapore Slings, except Dorian who ordered his usual sparkling water. He said alcohol caused wrinkles. Wrinkles were the last thing on my twenty-one-year-old mind as I sipped on my drink slowly trying to make it last. Looking across the room, I stared again into the sea of green-eyed pleasure that would soon be my sorrow.

Chanel asked, "Who's that guy looking at us?"

"That one's mine," I said matter-of-factly.

"He looks like trouble anyway, Bonnie." Chanel gave me the second sign. I ignored that one, too.

Dorian threw his hands up, 'Not my type."

Frankie was this tall, handsome red man who wooed me hard that night. Buying me rum and cokes and chicken wing appetizers until my stomach protruded noticeably in my tight dress. Although I was petite, my behind didn't know it. I squeezed it into the size seven anyway, thinking to myself, Spandex *is supposed to expand*.

Nonetheless, Frankie made me laugh at his jokes, and stories about his life growing up as a foster child. I noticed the dimples on his cheeks when he smiled. I also saw a bit of sadness in his eyes.

He said. "Not knowing who you are, or where you come from, allow you to create who you would like to be."

It was kind of sad in one way, but he seemed to have had a pretty good handle on life. I enjoyed getting to know him that night. At least that part of him he exposed. I made up my mind that he was the one. My heart soon went along with it.

Three months into our love, the rumors began to ebb and flow like the tidewaters on Myrtle Beach in February. Sometimes grins followed the jeers and whispers. At other times the gossip waters were so high, I could barely escape them. "Bonnie, he's married," Chanel said. "With three small children." Her words of advice and comfort, "I'm just looking out for you, Cuz," found deaf ears.

Frankie told me about his marriage the night we met. That was always one of my probes before getting too comfortable with a man. I checked his left hand for a ring or a ring line. Then I asked, "Is there a Mrs. Frankie running around somewhere?"

"Not now," he had replied. He had married a woman who was eight years older than him. He was eighteen, just emancipated from foster care. He said emancipated meant you were a man, so to prove it, he got a job, a wife with a ready-made family. "We were together off and on for two years. And the kids, three of them, are not mine, although I had taken care of them like they were. Hell, the oldest one was eight when I married her. That would've meant I was out there doing the nasty when I was 10 years old. I'm bad and all that. But I aint that bad," He laughed. "I finally divorced her about six months ago." He added, "The woman was a little crazy. But I do miss the kids."

I never asked him about that again. What he told me, I believed. I commended him for being fatherly. Janel didn't say too much about my romance with Frankie. She'd shake her head when his name was mentioned, though. She gave him an evil look once or twice when he came to see me or pick me up. I ignored all of it. The whispers, the laughs, even the looks of pity that came when someone dared eye contact. Mama surprised me. She said nothing good or bad. Not that she eagerly approved; more like, she had taught me all she could about life, now the rest was up to me. One bright spot came from my grandma. "Honey," she said. "Don't let anyone tell you who to love. We all have to deal with love on our own terms. Besides, I think you can make a good man out of him." Grandma had wisdom, so no one else's bad review of Frankie mattered.

Moving in together and setting up house proved petrifying and comforting all at the same time. Three months was fast, but I was on my way to happiness. We bought extravagant furniture on a too-long installment plan. Frankie's credit was "not established" so I put everything in my name. Even the one-bedroom apartment lease had only my name on it. "We'll change it to both our names when we get married," he said.

Frankie lost his job at the car dealership within the month. "Consistent low sales." Everyone goes through a slump. His was three months straight. He said, "I saved up enough money that we can live on until something else comes along."

That was good enough for me. But nothing came along. Nothing. I went to work and left Frankie home in bed each day the sun came up. Yes, I worked Monday through Sunday (I had to get a part-time job at Wal-Mart), trying to keep lights on and our (my) furniture from being placed on the sidewalk. I saw some of the money that he had saved up. He bought groceries, paid a bill or two. The rest he blew on rims for his car. He did go looking for work on some days, but when his unemployment money started coming in, he settled in. When I came home from work, he would be gone. Sometimes I wouldn't see him or his red convertible BMW until the next day. He'd come back smelling like liquor and nightclub, explaining with one of his many excuses that always ended the same, "It was too late for me to drive home. Besides, I was drinking so I crashed at a friend's house."

"What friend?" I'd yell. "A phone call would have kept me from worrying."

He'd walk right back out the door until the next morning, "Where were you all night," became a constant interrogation in the bleak existence we called our home. I would *blow up*. A punch or two always followed by him or by me. He always hit harder. Note to self. *Don't hit this fool.*

Many nights I'd ride around our small town looking for some semblance of him. His car. Soon, when he did come home, we would fight for me not "minding my damn business."

"I thought you were my damn business." I'd cry.

He'd say, "I'm sorry."

I said, "Why are you sorry, Frankie?"

SILENCE was his reply. Frankie had said he was sorry so much, I started calling him Mr. Sorry. I believed Frankie loved me the best he knew how. Even though I suspected that he was cheating on me, I never caught him. Frankie promised me that he wasn't. I suspected he sold drugs, too. Then I caught myself. Drug dealers have money. What little money Frankie had gone into his car, I figured. Paying Wells Fargo Bank and Liberty Mutual Insurance every month took all of his unemployment checks.

We fought over everything. I didn't like what Frankie cooked for dinner most nights, so I complained, "Hot dogs and baked beans, again?"

We fought if he didn't like what I wore to work. "That skirt is a too damn short; who are you dressing for at work?"

Before we made love and after love, we fought, but the love was our glue. Sweaty flesh and moaning in the middle of the night or day became a panacea. And like one of those old sad blues songs, my heart struck chords of splendor and despair all at the same time.

After months of going through hell just to enjoy a little heaven, I changed the locks on the apartment door. Phone calls went unanswered on both sides. Our love was finally over. Silly me! Love doesn't let you decide when it's over.

Frankie bang continuously on the front door in the middle of heat filled night, cussing and crying, "Open the damn door." Neighbors, who no doubt, had tired of the interminable turbulences that often ripped through the small apartment building, called the police. He had left before they arrived, so I was stuck talking to them. Explaining! Trying to keep "the man" out of our business, I told them, I didn't know who had made that loud noise. "I wondered about all that racket myself."

Unable to convince them that I was just an innocent bystander of such goings on, one of the officers admonished harshly, "Get a restraining order, Ma'am." I didn't want a restraining order; I didn't want Frankie restrained. I just wanted him to be who I had in my head.

Separation from Frankie for that long made me a little crazy. Mainly, when I would see him at the Bony Room. Each time, he had a new girl on his arm. Always pretty. Dorian begged me not approach Frankie that night. "You know y'all gon start fighting," he said.

Of course, my heart ignored him. "Who is this," I yelled before throwing a drink in his face.

"None of your business," He said wiping his face with the sleeve of his shirt. And if you throw another drink in my face you gon be sorry."

I understood when Frankie was serious, so I just kept yelling and cussing at him AND the tramp he was with until the manager threw all of us out the club.

Nevertheless, his actions were no more sensible than mine. One night, while leaving the movies with a mixed group of co-workers, he approached us. Frankie saw me go into the theater with one of the guys from work. Waiting for me on the sidewalk, Frankie grabbed me by the shoulders. "I caught you," he said pushing me against the wall.

"What are you talking about," I yelled.

"You know what the hell I'm talking about. You and this Negro you been with."

My friends (if I could call them friends) walked away hurriedly, out of sight.

Embarrassed, I broke free and pushed him. Hard. Frankie lost his footing on the cracked pavement, falling to the sidewalk backward. His head hit the pavement, knocking him unconscious. I screamed, "Call 911."

Bystanders called for, what I thought, an ambulance, but both police and ambulance sirens screamed through the brightly lit streets while I kneeled down cradling Frankie in my arms until he regained consciousness.

We both went to jail that night. Fortunately, no charges were filed against us. One of my co-workers had told the police that we were all playing around, and Frankie slipped and fell. They hadn't left me after all. I found out later, they had just moved across the street to get a good seat for the *Frankie and Bonnie Show.* Thank God for favors.

After that night, I let him back in the apartment. He promised he would change. "Change what?" I asked him. The funny thing, Frankie didn't know what he was doing wrong. I found out later that he never gave up his apartment when we "moved in together." When I asked him why, he just said, one of his foster parents had told him that shacking up wasn't the right thing to do. If you love a woman, you marry her, and not just live with her. He figured that if he maintained his own residence, it would be like sleeping over rather than shacking up.

Yes! He did love me. On his terms. Some asked why I stayed on those terms. What a strange question. He was my love. Sometimes a broken promise doesn't matter when love is involved. With love, you must wait. Some of us understand that. Many don't. Love is neither good nor bad, it just is. It has nothing to do with you or me. It is an entity in itself. Be careful, it will devour the weak. If we are fortunate, it will leave us and take on another host. For many, it can linger like an open sore, and ooze like pus. But a sore eventually heals. Never mind that it will crust over and leave a scar.

Loving Frankie was not my doing. Sad thing, too, love makes you want for it. I wanted love too much. Sometimes it felt like drowning. Unable to breathe. Other times, it was paradise. I found that love warrants patience. Patience? Perhaps. But what clinched the deal with Frankie and me? **Me**… running him over with his BMW to receive his love on equal terms. After a few skin grafts and physical therapy, Frankie was back on the job, selling Toyotas by day, and doing light janitorial work by night. His left leg still drags a bit causing a slight limp, but that hasn't lessened the love we share. The twins came less than a year ago, after our wedding. What I found to be true, however... love aint nobody's friend. It is merely Mother Nature's intimidation, for us to reproduce; insisting that we continue this obligatory existence, we call life. And who can say 'no' to Mother Nature?

Hogging All the Love

Another party for Mrs. Anna Hillstrom. This one made the fifth birthday party for the ninety-nine-year-old woman that week. Anna delighted in all of the adoring attention, and she proved to be still full of life and as vibrant as a new bride. The Park Street Neighborhood Association brought her cake and flowers. Yellow tulips were her favorite. The new neighbors heard the lively singing and laughter from across the street, and they joined the others.

Anna's children gave her the first party the Saturday evening before. Just about everyone came. Sons and daughters, in-laws, grandchildren, and their children, other relatives, and friends, all made their way to the grand celebration. They had to rent the Bridgeton Hall for such a large gathering. Delicious food, music, dancing, and lively conversation. They all thought she would skip the festivities that Friendship Baptist Church had planned for her on that Sunday afternoon, but Anna delighted in that one, too.

The Senior Travelers Club and the Park Street Center followed suit with sprightly get-togethers on

Monday and again on Tuesday both in her honor. The festivities finally came to a close with just the close neighbors. Miss Anna enjoyed all the loving kindness of the people on her street, smiling with every greeting card and neatly wrapped present placed in front of her. Each show of affection added more light to Anna's eyes. Someone whispered to another partygoer, "I think Miss Anna will live to see one hundred."

"Or longer."

Yes, there was no sitting down for this near centenarian. Anna still drove a car, which by the way was no antique. She believed in keeping up with the times, so she bought a late model sedan of no notable significance other than it was a shiny light blue. "No dull grays or blacks," she had informed the impatient salesman.

Three months passed and the once green leaves on the maple and oak trees throughout Bridgeton now displayed gold and orange tapestry, particularly on old Park Street. Yet another birthday shone on the horizon. Mrs. Ellen Murray turned ninety-nine that breezy morning. Like Anna Hillstreet, she had lived on the same street for over fifty years.

Miss Ellen sat among the fallen leaves that covered every inch of the wooden porch. Sporadically, she rocked back and forth in one of the splintered old rocking chairs humming gospel songs way down low. The rocker added a sweet melodious undertone as the leaves cracked underneath.

Arthritic hands folded over one another resting in an aproned lap. Miss Ellen watched as indifferent neighbors and strangers passed by her house, some nodding greetings, others unaware of the old lady's presence.

"Good morning, Sister." Mrs. Anna Hillstrom's soft, pleasant voice echoed in the breeze as she walked up the four wooden steps, arms full.

"Good morning to you, Sister," replied Miss Ellen. An unhappy face all of a sudden dressed up in a bright smile. "I've been waiting for you."

"I know, I know," Anna said. She placed the neatly wrapped gift and a greeting card on the table that separated the rocking chairs and joined Miss Ellen in humming.

"You want some tea?"

"Don't I always," Anna answered.

"Well come on in the house," Miss Ellen motioned for Anna. "You have to excuse the mess."

"What mess you talking about?" Miss Anna asked, "Your house is just as lovely as it's always been."

"Thank you, Sister."

The ladies enjoyed hot morning tea with lemon while reminiscing about the good old days of husbands, children, and life before time and age invaded and took family and friends away. Soon, a light tap on the front door interrupted the sparkling conversation.

"Who could that be?" Miss Ellen asked.

"I'll go see," Anna replied as she wasted no time getting to the door.

To Miss Ellen's surprise, Anna returned with a large store-bought birthday cake in hand, and about twenty of their neighbors, singing the Happy Birthday song with cheerful voices.

Through laughter and warm hugs, Miss Ellen cried tears of happiness. She was speechless and could only smile with her hands planted on both sides of her face. In all her years on Park Street, the neighbors had never formally celebrated her birthday. For the past twenty years, her birthdays had been spent with Anna enjoying hot tea and warm conversation. She wondered why out of the blue the neighbors came there for her birthday. "It's not like I just turned one hundred," she managed to speak finally, with joy-filled eyes.

With a burst of laughter, Anna hugged Miss Ellen, saying, "Some people just like hogging all the love, now don't they? Happy birthday, Sister."

Wearing a broad smile, Miss Ellen said, "Thank you so much for this wonderful party."

"You are quite welcome," Anna Hillstrom replied. She had enjoyed more than enough parties of her own that year. Family and friends had lavished her with so much love, she didn't want to hog all the love from her best friend. "This turned out to be the best party yet."

Someone else whispered to another partygoer, "I think Miss Ellen will live to see one hundred."

Another whispered, "Or longer."

The Candy Store Owner

Back in 1961, in the small town of Lambert, there lived an old man whose name, even now, is too creepy to say aloud, so I'm going to whisper it to you. *Mr. Livermore.* No first name. At least we never heard of one. Actually, we never heard him speak at all. He just pushed out a grunt and a nod.

Ironically, this scary old man owned the only candy store in the neighborhood. And you know how much kids love candy. This store had the best penny candies a child's meager allowance could afford. Squirrel Nuts and Mary Janes, Sugar Daddies, Baby Ruth, and other chocolate covered candy bars that were sure to rot out our teeth before puberty. Large apothecary-like jars accommodated the assortment of loose cookies – coconut and lemon bars, and such – two for one cent. What a bargain! Those cookies were a big seller for us children and the teenagers who could most likely find a penny just by walking down the street. The old humming freezer with the see-through top kept the Popsicles and Ice cream sandwiches just the right temperature in summer and winter. And we ate them year-round.

The treats were our treasure. Even though the store was always pristine, *Mr. Livermore* wasn't. The curly gray hair on his head and face was forever in need of a trim. He dressed in a tattered old green army jacket that covered the nub where his left hand used to be. He had a noisy peg leg, too. I guess that's what triggered his rigidity uneven gait. CLICK CLACK! CLICK CLACK! CLICK CLACK! The sound resonated on the store's gray cement floor as the old man moved around filling our orders of sweet and tasty delights.

The grown folks told us not to 'pick at' Mr. Livermore. They said he deserved respect since he lost both his hand and leg in the First World War. But we got the *real* story from some of the older neighborhood kids that went like this:

> Late one muggy summer night, a neighborhood boy named Willie Lee, leisurely walked down the Union Street railroad tracks. Just moments earlier, Willie Lee had been at the coal and icehouse where he'd been relaxing by the big blocks of ice, drinking a Nehi orange soda. As he strolled the tracks, Willie Lee sucked boiled peanuts from their shells as he had done countless times before,

tossing them in his path. The moon was bright, and the mosquitos were biting. All of a sudden, Willie Lee heard something or someone close behind him. The sound of freshly nailed taps on the heels of some big shoes went CLICK CLICK! CLICK CLICK! Nearing his house, Willie Lee began to walk faster. The faster he walked, the louder and faster the CLICK CLICK! CLICK CLICK! CLICK CLICK! CLICK CLICK! Willie Lee looked back, and in the shadows was Old Man Livermore heading towards him. CLICK CLICK! CLICK CLICK! CLICK CLICK! CLICK CLICK! Livermore ran faster and faster towards Willie Lee. Suddenly, two great big hands grabbed hold of Willie Lee's long skinny neck from behind. Tighter and tighter, the old man's grip persisted. After a while, Willie Lee proved to be smarter and stronger than Mr. Livermore. Willie Lee bent his right leg and provided Mr. Livermore with a hard kick to the shin. He broke free from the old man's mean clutches that had nearly taken his life. They tussled like two bulls on those old Southern railroad tracks. Neither wanting to give up. Neither wanting to go on. Soon, the dark, gloomy night lit up like a Friday night football field. They heard the loud whistling of that old locomotive. As the rumbling of the tracks moved closer and closer towards them, the fight intensified. The old man pushed and pulled at Willie Lee. But Willie Lee returned the favor. Thrusting his knee into Willie Lee's stomach, the old man was determined not to give in. Unexpectedly, Willie Lee loosened his grip on Mr. Livermore. The old man's eyes showed a glimmer of victory, but Willie Lee came back with a two-piece karate chop to the old man's neck. The potency of Willie Lee's Okinawan sting knocked the old man down on the tracks. He twisted and turned, struggling to get up as the powerful train drew nearer. As fate intervened, the old man slipped on Willie Lee's slimy boiled peanuts that had fallen during the struggle. As fate would intervene a second time, the fast-moving train ran right over Mr. Livermore, cutting off his left hand and his right leg. It was said that Willie Lee was the first victim to get away alive. As the rest of the story goes, other children who walked that old track on a muggy summer night were not as lucky and are still missing to this day.

Even though Mr. Livermore was well-known among us young ones as the infamous railroad track killer, we were regular customers at that candy store anyway. As soon as money came our way, we were more than eager to part with it. A few cents here and there allowed our tummies immeasurable satisfaction. Keep in mind, not one of us kids ever went to the store alone. If one of us got a craving, and we had a few pennies to spend, we waited for another sweet-toothed cohort to tag along.

Late one Saturday on a hot summer day, a few of us neighborhood kids got on our bikes and rode to the store for ice cream. To our surprise, the old man wasn't there. In fact, the handwritten sign on the door read, "On Vacation." We knew what that meant. The old man was at it again. At least that's what the older neighborhood kids told us.

I never found out if Mr. Livermore ever killed again. The following week, my family moved across town. Another candy store owner lived in our new neighborhood. My older sister told me that same killer story. She said all candy store owners are killers by nature. I didn't believe her this time. The candy store owner in our new neighborhood was Mrs. Aubrey, my first-grade teacher. She was old, too but she had the sweetest smile of all the teachers at Lambert Elementary. Plus, she always put extra Mary Janes in my candy bag.

I often wondered about Livermore, though. When I returned years later, a new sign hand painted rested on the door, "OUT OF BUSINESS"! No one knew what happened to the old man, but who's to say he didn't just pack up and move to a new town with his alluring sweet treats. A word of warning, however; when you pass the Union Street railroad tracks late at night, you had better speed up. Mr. Livermore still walks those tracks late at night. If you pay close attention, you can hear him. CLICK CLACK! CLICK CLACK! CLICK CLACK! At least that's what the teenagers are saying.

BONUS STORY

Excerpted from *SOULS ON FIRE (Four Stories)*

One Hot Summer

They have eyes full of adultery, insatiable for sin. They entice unsteady souls ... **2 Peter 2:14 ESV**

It was Tamara's first summer away from Glen and the boys. The long Amtrak ride to New York was exhausting, but she welcomed it brimming with enthusiasm.

"Finally, some time for me," she said aloud, not caring if the stranger sitting next to her thought she was losing her mind.

Tamara yawned, swinging her arms high up over her head as to release the disquiet that had constrained her spirit for the past five years. Calm showed on her face as she gazed out the window at the dark towns speeding pass her. The noisy rumble of the tracks didn't disturb her as she relaxed to the inharmonious sounds. She tilted the seat back as far as she could without getting a nudge from the passenger sitting behind her and fell asleep, only waking up to make use of the tiny bathroom at the end of the car. Tamara was unaware of the frequent stops and hops through the cities and towns that called out to her in her dreams. For the first time in a long while, Tamara relaxed. There were no Sominex sleep aid and herb tea recipes from her sister. Just sleep - the way God intended. Neither the boarding nor the unloading passengers, nor the rising of the sun seemed to disturb her peace.

"Penn Station! Penn Station!" A husky voice came tunneling through the train's loudspeaker.

Tamara faintly heard the Pullman as she struggled to wake up. The well dressed, old man sitting next to her smiled as he elbowed her. "This is New York, Miss Lady. Are you getting off here?"

"Oh, yes. Thank you." Tamara said while wiping sleep drool from the corner of her mouth and wondered if she had been snoring loudly or making other embarrassing noises in her sleep. She could smell the unpleasantness of her own foul breath, remembering that she had sucked down her last breath mint a couple of hours earlier.

The Hotel Pennsylvania was across the street from the train station. She had made reservations months earlier, even before Glen knew of her trip. Tamara had asked her sister to join her on Thursday, and they could spend the rest of the week together doing the "New York thing" they had often joked about. The thought of a week of irresponsibility made her laugh out loud. She gathered her three suitcases from the platform, wondering if she had brought enough clothes for the weeklong stay. As she made her way through the rushing crowd of travelers, she thought, *Did I bring my…* Tamara reached into the side zipper of her oversized bag and felt her wallet resting securely in place. She scrambled erratically around the bottom touching everything from keys and lipstick to a twisted stick of Big Red chewing gum that she quickly peeled and placed in her mouth. What she didn't find was the small medicine bag that carried her *mercy medicines* – Ativan! Dexatrim! Deprofin! Pills that kept her sane. The Ativan she could do without as long as she didn't get *unnerved*. One reason for the *getaway* was to relax. Dexatrim could be bought from any bonafide drug store anywhere in America. The *Depro* was different. She had to stay on schedule with her birth control pills. She was too fertile to miss one day, let alone a week. She remembered last year.

Deciding to give her body a break from the toxins, Tamara fasted from all medicines for two months. Although she had used her diaphragm, pregnancy was inescapable – and impractical. She never said a word about it, not even to Glen. One chilly morning in late September, she left home expecting and returned home, not. Tamara asked for God's forgiveness and swore she'd never do it again, ever.

Madison Square Garden! She gazed up and around at the great big towering buildings. The glaring sun distorted the images, and she imagined the tall buildings staring down at her. She felt like Jack in the land of the giants. The noisy city streets were packed full of weird and wonderful people who looked right through each other as they passed. It was seven-thirty and the evening breeze was only hinting. The pavement was still hot as the street vendors beckoned her to purchase T-shirts and other miscellaneous items from their makeshift kiosks lined on the avenues. New Yorkers and people from all over the world bustled through the crowded streets without even the slightest insinuation of eye contact. Seventh Avenue was full of activity, and Tamara carefully crossed over with luggage in tow. What Tamara had on her mind was neither the loud noise of the idling taxicab backed up in traffic nor the blaring siren of fire truck trying to get past but kicking off her high heels and settling down to a steaming hot bubble bath.

Checking into the hotel was quick and painless. "Room 938, Ms. Williams. Do you need help with your luggage?" The hotel clerk asked as he placed her American Express card and magnetic door key in her hand.

No thanks, but can you tell me how to get to the elevator?"

Pointing straight ahead, he said, "Go out this way; turn left, go towards the entrance, then turn to your right. You'll see them. Next." He immediately dismissed Tamara as though she was as inconsequential as the card key he had just given her.

Hotel Pennsylvania was an old picturesque, almost baroque building; like the pictures, she'd seen on her grandfather's postcards hanging over the bureau chest in his bedroom. It was decorated with old furniture; at least that's what Tamara got for her eighty dollars a night. Her single room was too small and too narrow. It housed one single bed. White and gold French Provincial style, pushed too close against a wall. A tiny night table sat by the bed holding an old marble-based candlestick lamp, an alarm clock radio, and a television remote control that was connected to the table with a flexible line, similar to a telephone cord. The small matching dresser was lower to the floor than the ones she was used to. It had three drawers, and a mirror of the same width bolted to the wall. A brass-plated bench with a cream-colored leather seat was sprawled at the foot of the bed directly across from a television that sat bolted to a small stand in front of a tall single window. Tamara thought it odd that there was no window screen in place. Thick sun faded, jacquard drapes that matched a green bedspread embellished the decor. The bathroom was small with a white porcelain footed bathtub that complemented the oval-shaped pedestal sink. The entire room had a tender stale odor that gave it character. Though it was not what Tamara had expected or been used to, she was by no means offended. She kicked off her shoes and fell spread eagle on the small bed, dropping fast to sleep.

The alarm clock sounded at six o'clock in the morning. Although she couldn't remember setting it, it was the right time. Tamara couldn't believe she had slept through the night. Then she remembered the seventeen-hour train ride from South Carolina. Stiff and achy, she realized that her customary morning shower had to be replaced with the full-fledged bubble bath she had missed the night before.

As she lay nearly roasting in a full tub of hot foaming bubbles, she thought about the intense argument with Glen the night before:

> "Why all of a sudden have you decided that you need to go to New York," he had said part disgusted and part surprised.
>
> "It's not all of a sudden." Tamara had answered evasively making Glen even angrier and more suspicious.
>
> He'd yelled, "What about the boys?"
>
> "What about them? You'll be here. Spend some time with them." She'd yelled back, though not as loud and with not as much ire. "Y'all can do that male bonding thing you're always doing with your friends on Friday night."
>
> "Tamara, this aint like you. What's going on?"
>
> "Nothing! I thought about this for a long time, and I decided I wanted to go. What's the big deal?" Tamara knew what the big deal was. She had never been apart from her children for more than a day. Then she had snuck her plans into an idle conversation just a week earlier.

What are we supposed to do for a whole two weeks?" Glen had calmed down.

"One week! And you'll do what you have to do. The boys will be at camp all day, and when you leave work, you can pick them up, feed them, and do the same thing I do every day. Entertain them." Tamara sighed, "Dog, Glen, it's just a week. It's not like I'm going around the world."

Glen said. "Sounds to me like you got something up your sleeve and it aint just an arm."

They'd fallen asleep without saying goodnight. Without making love.

Three hundred or so Toastmasters from all over the state had congregated in the large conference room. It was evident by the engaging chatter that many of them either knew each other or had gotten acquainted at the reception the night before - the one Tamara had slept through. Connie and Jeanine, two members of her local club, were the only people she recognized, and she made her way to the back of the room to greet them.

The food from the continental breakfast was just about gone when she arrived at the long buffet table. She picked up half of a bagel that had been toasted with butter and quickly stuffed it in her mouth then attempted to chase it down with a small glass of orange juice. "Good morning." A familiar voice beckoned her from behind.

Slowly turning, she tried to avoid being seen chewing on hard bread. Her heart increased beats when she recognized the man who had startled her. She hadn't seen him since Flint, Michigan thirteen years earlier. Tamara thought of how handsome he still looked, and she smiled.

"Paul Reddick?" She flung her arms around him. "What are you doing up here?"

He returned the affection with a tight hug around her waist that lifted her from the floor.

Without releasing the firm grip on his shoulders, she thought of how pleasing his arms felt around her. "Put me down before you drop me!" Tamara said laughing so hard her shoe slipped off.

"How have you been, Tamara?" he said gradually lowering her back to the floor.

"I've been good. What have you been up to, Paul?" She noticed that he still wore Aramis cologne and it smelled just as pleasant on him as it did before.

"Same ol' thing. That's about it. I transferred to the Atlanta Office about six years ago. What about you? What have you been up to?"

"I taught over in Inkster for a couple of years, and then I moved back down South, got married, had some babies. You know. Stuff. I'm still teaching."

"Well, you still look good, Tam. Damn good."

Tamara blushed. "You do too." She wondered if he was married. "Are you here with your wife?"

"I'm divorced" He responded like he was proud of it.

"Oh, I'm sorry to hear that," she said, but she wasn't sorry. *No woman deserved a man like Paul Reddick.*

"I'm not," he said slightly grinning.

The seats that were empty moments earlier were filling up quickly. The Toastmaster of the Day headed towards the microphone, signaling for the start of the meeting.

"Oh, the session is about to start. I'll see you around." Tamara went to the front of the conference room where Connie Willingham had saved her a place in one of the perfectly aligned padded chairs beside her.

Paul followed. "Let's have lunch. There's a charming little Jewish deli about a block from the hotel. I hear they make a mean Rueben. Meet me after the morning session so we can catch up."

"Okay! I'll see you after the session." *Charming?* She remembered how pretentious he was, and she laughed to herself.

"Who is that gorgeous hunk of flesh?" Connie asked as she watched him stroll to the back of the room.

"Just a friend I hadn't seen in years."

"Well, you better be very careful with Mr. Just A Friend. He looks like he can be more trouble than he's worth." Connie was almost smiling.

Paul returned to the back of the conference room and sat next to a young woman waiting for him.

Tamara considered Paul's invitation while she remembered their brief, but steamy courtship thirteen summers ago:

The distinction of being the lone black, straight, and available male at Michigan Property and Casualty Insurance Company made Paul Reddick an enigma. He had dressed in nicely tailored business suits and strutted around the fifth-floor office like a rooster in a hen house. Tamara, as well as most of the women in the office, knew he was full of himself; all the same, he was fine. And when you're twenty-one, fine is at the top of the list of male qualifications, second only to financial - and the two were interchangeable depending on the degree of either. He had chosen Tamara to wine and dine exclusively for two months. She had fallen passionately in love with this man who made her soul ache just thinking about him. Then suddenly, without a warning, Paul broke off the affair. No real explanation! Just, *I have some things going on in my life that I need to sort out. Alone.* Despite a broken heart torn into small bits, she somehow managed to piece it back together long enough to finish the last days of her summer internship with dignity – rationalizing that through the whole of their brief liaison, Paul had treated her special. Although that was the last time she saw him until now, their romance had often popped up in her head over the years.

What caused Paul to suddenly lose interest then and more significantly, what was his subtle interest in her now? To Tamara's amazement, he embraced the same cool, calm, and collected manner he had when she last saw him. Except for the graying around his temples and his thick mustache, Paul hadn't aged at all. He was still beautiful. She wondered what made some men retain their youthful vigor and others just plain go to the dogs. Glen had really let himself go; gaining more weight than he openly admitted. His blue jeans had begun to fit snugly under a quietly protruding belly and rode high up on his butt. He had refused to buy a larger size, buying a Walk Fit Exerciser instead that was standing in the garage gathering more dust than miles. Tamara was comparing them, her old lover to her new love; there was no comparison. Even considering Glen's indifference, he had, after all, been a good provider. And he loved her.

"Up and at it, you guys," Glen said summoning the boys from a peaceful sleep.

Mondays are bad enough, but I have to play Mr. Mom, too, he thought.

The boys' clothes had been organized for the five days she'd be away. Shorts, shirts, shoes, and everything else she thought they'd need for the week were hung neatly in the closet. Placed on each set of clothes were labels with names and the days of the week. Socks and underwear were neatly tagged and arranged in the heavy oak chest of drawers. Notes Tamara had written rested carefully on top of them. It couldn't have been any easier. All the same, Glen felt it his duty to complain.

Jamal, the oldest, was tall and curious. He carried Tamara's tiny bone structure and her tense personality. At nine years old, he was an avid sports enthusiast. Tamara had engaged him in every sport available in their middle-class community. Soccer and Pee Wee football were his favorites. Tradeoffs were played with neighboring parents, transporting him and the other children to practices and games. She was glad it was summer since no sports team demanded her time. Summer also meant that school was out. She was relieved of the natural sounds of small voices calling her name, except those of her own boys. Tamara had taught kindergarten for the past eleven years. She never regretted switching her major from Business to Early Childhood Education. The career adjustment wasn't a noble choice, but one of selfish motivation. Tamara viewed teaching as a way to enjoy three months of summer and every major U.S. holiday. She had no interest in overtime or corporate politics. The problem was Glen didn't share the same aspirations.

His job at Centergy Computer Corporation became more demanding as time passed. Although Tamara maneuvered as much free time away from work as she needed, the opposite was true for Glen. His job commanded long hours, and he was on-call more than off. When he did manage to get a day away from the office, his time was generally consumed with home repairs, television (mainly sports), and sleep.

"Daddy, what's in here to eat?" Hakim asked, wiping the sleep from his eyes.

"I don't know. Wash up, and I'll see."

Hakim was the left half of twins and older than Bashir by nearly two minutes. Although identical, Glen and Tamara encouraged their individuality. At seven, they were hard, rough boys and bigger than average, who consumed their weight in food and couldn't get enough of football and wrestling. "Let's see you guys." Glen said as he pulled packages from the pantry, "We got Pop Tarts. Who wants Pop Tarts?"

"Not me!"

The twins followed with, "Me neither."

"Okay, what about some Frankenberry?"

"That's not Frankenberry," Bashir said laughing.

"Yes, it is," Glen pulled the box of cereal from the shelf.

Hakim snickered loudly, rocking back and forth. "No, Daddy. That's not."

"Well, what is it?" He brought the box up close to his face as though he was missing something obvious.

"That's Monsterberry," Jamal joined his brothers in the laughter.

"Monsterberry, huh. So, your Mama pulled the old switcheroo on you guys again."

"Yeah. And Mama think we don't know, but we saw the Monsterberry box in the garbage can." Bashir steady giggling.

"Let's not tell her we know, okay. When she asked why we're not eating it, we'll tell her, we're trying to cut back on sugar."

The laughter grew louder as the boys moved back and forth in the chairs. They took satisfaction in the camaraderie they had developed with Glen.

"I know, I know, we can eat some grits, with sausage, eggs, and pancakes," Hakim said excitedly.

"Um, that might take a longer time to fix than we have," Glen said, knowing he wouldn't even attempt to cook breakfast. He prided himself on not cooking. Not that he viewed food preparation as woman's work; he just didn't want to set a precedent in the kitchen. Most of his friends had complained that when their wives found out they could cook, they were given dinner menus to prepare food on a regular basis. Glen had escaped that task for twelve years, and he wasn't about to go down now. "Let's go to McDonald's and get the Big Breakfast."

"YES!" Hakim and Jamal rushed to the garage pushing each other, competing on who rides shotgun in the SUV.

"Hurry up, you guys. I got to take you all the way across town and then go to work." Glen said as he motioned for Hakim to get in the back with Bashir.

"Ah, man! Why do we have to go to camp?" Hakim shrugged his shoulders and pouted. He pulled a basketball from under the back seat and proceeded to twirl it around on his chubby fingers.

"Because I have to go to work."

The drive-thru window at McDonald's was crowded. The boys persuaded Glen to let them go inside to order breakfast. He knew that once inside, they would want to eat inside. Probably play, too.

Hakim and Bashir quickly scoffed down hot cakes and sausage and ran out the glass back door to the large play area.

"Come on, you guys. I told you I was in a hurry. I got to take you to camp and go to work. I'm already late," Glen called loudly over the crowd of children leisurely mixing in the fishnet-lined box filled with plastic balls.

"Daddy," Jamal whined. "We can stay home by ourselves. Camp sucks."

"Watch your mouth."

"I'm old enough to be in charge of these two."

"I can be in charge of myself." Bashir raised his head through the sea of red, blue, green, and yellow balls.

"Me too."

Thump!

"Ouch! Stop! Daddy, Jamal thumped my head."

119

The plastic ball Bashir threw from the pin to retaliate against Jamal missed and hit Glen.

They laughed.

It was eight forty-five. The drive to camp was fifteen minutes away. It would take another twenty minutes to get to Centergy. Glen thought about calling the office to let them know he would be late. Instead, he thought, *I got vacation time I can take.* "Who wants to go to Carowinds?"

"Me!"

"Me! Me! Me!"

"Are you for real, Daddy?" Bashir asked, unsure if he believed him.

"Yeah! Why not? I need to run by the office and pick up some files. I can work from the house when we get back. Besides, I hadn't eaten one of those big old fat Italian Sausage Dogs in ages.

"How do they taste Daddy?"

"They taste greasy, Jamal," Glen said, laughing.

Jamal thought about his mother. Tamara took them on spontaneous trips to the beach or the thirty-mile trip to Grandpa's just because it was summer. They had taken a family vacation to Orlando's Magic Kingdom year before last, but Glen brought work with him and turned it into a working vacation. Tamara had made that vacation fun. "I wish Mama was here so she can come with us."

"Nope!" Glen said, "This is just us guys this week. We'll give her a call later."

♀

The New York air was hot. Not like the muggy heat of the south, but dry and roasting. While waiting to meet Paul when (or if) he arrived, Tamara enjoyed the coolness of the air-conditioned lobby at the Hotel Pennsylvania. She halfway wanted him to *stand her up*, unsure if she should dig up those old dry bones from the past. Unfaithfulness had never occurred to Tamara. What harm is there in meeting an old friend for lunch? No doubt, Glen had become a bore, but she wasn't the energetic twenty-two-year-old graduate student he had married either.

"Hey, Lady, been waiting long?" Paul sat on the thick cushioned sofa across from Tamara, startling her.

"No, not really, but I'm as hungry as a horse." She had actually been waiting thirty minutes and read nearly all of the *New York Times*. "Where is this deli?"

"Just a couple of blocks." He said as he stood up and reached for Tamara's hand.

Subconsciously, she pulled away. Not knowing where that sudden reaction came from, she recovered by pretending to lose her balance.

"Are you okay?"

"Yeah, just a little dizzy." She lied. Tamara acknowledged the old feelings swelling back up inside of her. She felt that same tingling in her stomach she thought had abandoned her in her youth.

"Maybe, we shouldn't go. The heat is blazing out there, and I don't want you to pass out on me."

"Oh! I'll be all right. Let's go on to . . . What's the name of this place, again?"

Paul sat on the arm of the chair beside Tamara. "Are you sure? I can order something and have it sent to your room."

Why is he acting so sweet? Tamara thought. *It is so out of character unless something's in it for him. Maybe he's changed.* She laughed inside at the thought of such hardcore arrogance converting to quiet humility in one lifetime.

The sunrays streaming in through the tall lobby window cast sparkles in Paul's light brown eyes. Tamara thought of how handsome he was, and she wanted to kiss his large round strawberry lips. Placing one hand on the arm of the chair and the other on Paul's thigh, she stood up, strolled to the elevator, and called out to him over her shoulder, "I'll have something sent to my room."

"I'll join you."

The objection Tamara thought would flow easily from her lips did not make it past the knot in her stomach. It was replaced with a slow nod of her head. As she pressed the elevator button, Paul took hold of her hand. This time there was no resistance.

The hotel room was cold. Tamara had purposely left the air conditioner on full blast to stifle the musty odor.

"Come on in and have a seat." Tamara led Paul to the bench at the foot of the bed.

Paul sidestepped Tamara and headed to the bed realizing too late that it was lower to the floor than normal. He plopped down hard falling back. Pulling a pillow from underneath a neatly tucked bedspread, he strategically positioned it under his head.

I know what he's up to. I don't have any business in here with this man.

"Why are you way over there, Tamara? Come here and sit next to me." A crafty grin surfaced between cute dimples.

"Paul, I thought we were going to order lunch."

"We got plenty time to eat. Come here." He coolly patted a place on the bed next to him. "Come here."

Tamara proceeded to reach for the phone book on the night table, ignoring his gestures. As she tried to make her way past him, he grabbed her by the waist. "That's right. Come here."

The heat from his body excited her. She closed her eyes and selflessly let him guide her towards him. Resting on his thigh, she felt her body collapse on his. He pulled her closer, softly kissing her on the face and neck. His moist lips continued to travel exploiting her - inch by inch. Her mouth. Her eyes, down to the tip of her nose, to her neck, her cleavage and again to her welcoming mouth. Sweat assembled on her breasts and thighs as they heaved unevenly at each thrust of his tongue moving in and out of her mouth in rhythmic persuasion. A carnal appetite stronger than any cravings she had known before replaced the hunger that had lain awake in her stomach moments earlier. Any thought of propriety was suspended as she explored the realm of pleasure that had once been her conquest.

♂

This was the first time Glen had taken a day off work just to be with the boys - for fun, other than a planned vacation with the family. Even those vacations had been working ones. Other than sickness or school-related activities, they rarely did anything together. He soon realized that just being with the boys was nice. The kind of nice he felt when he saw them for the first time. Just out of the womb and slimy like freshly caught fish. He looked in the rearview mirror. It was like he hadn't seen them since they had grown up. Quiet, looking out the window at the trees and the billboards running down I-77. He was surprised to see all three boys content on the back seat not touching each other mischievously, the way they usually do for aggravation's sake. Instead, they sat silent and still. Jamal had his thumb in his mouth as he massaged the back of his ear - a clear indication that he would soon fall asleep.

It was better than noon when they arrived at the amusement park. The truck sighed relief, and the boys awoke with synchronized yawns that were loud and energetic.

"We're here?" Bashir said jumping to his feet and bumping the top of his head.

Jamal laughed, "You big dummy."

"No dumber than you, Jamal." Bashir returned, pushing Jamal in the stomach so hard almost knocking the wind out of him.

"Ok you guys, we can get back in the truck and head on back home."

"No, No. We won't fight." Hakim said in defense of his brothers, but more for his benefit. He was ready to ride the TOP GUN. It was the new roller coaster. None of his friends had ridden on it. He wanted to be the first one. He hoped the ride operator would give some *slack* and let him ride, even though he was less than five feet tall.

Hakim pushed Bashir out of the truck, "Come on, man. Behave so we won't have to go back home."

The admission to Carowinds cost a hundred and fifty dollars for all of them, even with the discount coupons he'd found in the newspaper. Glen asked the gatekeeper if the meals were included in the price of the tickets. He remembered when the price was less than twenty dollars each and cringed at how inflation had swelled over the years. He thought the increase was absurd, like college tuition. *These boys are gonna ride every freaking ride in this park whether they want to or not.*

"Jamal said a bad word, Daddy," Bashir said.

Jamal picked up a dried peach kernel from the pavement and threw it towards Bashir, missing him and hitting Glen in the back.

"DIDN'T I TELL YOU BOYS TO STOP ROUGHHOUSING? WE'RE GOING BACK TO 736 SYCAMORE IF I HAVE TO TELL YOU AGAIN!" Glen wasn't about to drive another eighty miles back home without going inside and getting his Italian Sausage Dog, and the boys knew it. They also knew he had just paid one hundred dollars to the young woman at the gate and he wasn't about to leave until he retrieved equal gratification.

The park was crowded with people of all persuasions. The lines to the rides were extra-long, and the boys ran in three different directions to wait their turn at the gigantic contraptions. "Get back here, you guys," Glen yelled. "We need to stay together."

"But I want to ride this," Hakim yelled back." He pointed to an enormous inverted steel machine with blazing letters. "TOP GUN."

"Okay. We'll ride this one first, and then someone else gets to pick the next one. Don't worry, we're gonna ride every last one of these rides, even if we have to stay here 'til the park closes. Or they kick us out!"

♀

On the outside, Tuesday morning was just like Monday morning. Blinding heat occupied the New York streets with pedestrians making their way minding their business. Taxicabs darted in and out of traffic jams; street vendors beckoned streetwalkers, many not acknowledging them. New York City had either opened early or never closed Monday night.

Yet, on the inside, Tuesday morning could never be the same as Monday. The air-conditioned hotel room could not stifle the odor of regret that had settled in the place where staleness once lived. The bedcovers laid spread out across the pale green carpet among two wine glasses that remembered the 1997 Ravenswood Zinfandel. Half eaten Reuben sandwiches rested between the bed and the night table calling out for redemption for being party to an act of failing.

Tamara stood naked, peering in the bathroom mirror at the stranger's reflection. Silence was the topic of the morning on the inside. Paul lay stretched out on the bare mattress of the small bed half asleep, all but naked on his back, covered only with black socks and victory. How did so many hours pass without her protest? Was it the mellowness of the wine that had clouded her judgment and her sense of moral responsibility? She could say that was why. Still, she chose a moment of excitement over a life's promise to someone else. She had ridden down that rutted road years ago. It was no more repaired now than then. What's more, it had dead-ended to a rocky cliff.

The person she saw in the mirror had her light brown eyes, her broad nose, and her thin mouth. Golden brown hair fell limp around a yellow-skinned face that looked like Tamara. The small sagging breasts that had once stood up proud before three babies and inertia took hold and the somewhat protruding stomach that still held the scars of two Caesareans were recognizable. Except, they wore the touch of a man that wasn't Glen Williams. With the rise of one single tear rolling solemnly down her cheek, Tamara was able to purge the stranger from the mirror and emerge to face that special Tuesday morning.

"Paul! Paul! Wake up. It's morning. You need to leave. It's morning." Tamara pushed and pulled the lump lying on the bed that wasn't real. If she admitted its existence, that would mean defeat. She wasn't defeated?

The triumphant co-conspirator rolled over; his feet touched the floor. He pulled his body up from the tainted bed and staggered in the bathroom. Tamara wrapped the wrinkled sheet tightly around her body as she watched the mirage standing, stretching, and yawning at the commode. The loud rushing sound of that masculine stream unnerved her. *Is it ever gonna finish its business*, she thought.

Finally, it ended. It walked out of the bathroom, uninhibited and full of its manhood.

"How about one for the road, Tam?"

It spoke!

She remembered those words well. There had been one for the road that night he broke off their romance. That seemed like yesterday to her now. Strange! She hadn't remembered that before. In all the years, she had not seen him, he really hadn't changed. His body was the same, and she realized he was the same man. He could disconnect himself from everything, even lovemaking. However, what they had made wasn't love. She loved Glen. What they had made felt like love, but it was lust – raw and primal lust. She looked down at his feet. The impermanence of a few moments of pleasure had displayed itself as it stood in only black ribbed socks. She wondered how such momentous passion could be turned on and off like an eye on a stove. At one moment so hot it could cause third-degree burns and minutes later, cold enough to touch barehanded and feel nothing. To him, she was a warm conquest - another night of corporeal release. They would part, and he would not remember. However, she would never forget. Not because of its special significance, but because of its ordinary insignificance. She was an adulterer, and she must burn in deep hell.

"Paul, get your clothes and leave. Please!"

"Come on. Just five minutes." He seized the sheet from her warm trembling body.

Tamara backed away, slower than she thought she wanted to. She didn't conceal her nakedness. Paul walked close to her. She wasn't surprised that she didn't resist his warm breath on her neck. Her body ached for him just like the many times before. Falling weak to his touch, she slipped deeper into the hell she had chosen.

Zinfandel had played no part in her failing this time, nor was she willing to accuse it. She was convinced that Paul was Satan and she was doomed to suffer eternal punishment in the fires of hell. However, for that Tuesday morning, she suffered the wanton pleasure of that fallen angel - over and over and over...

♂

With all their boasting, Carowinds had accepted the challenge and won. Glen and the boys hadn't conquered every ride in the amusement park; the Vortex closed as soon as they approached it. Two o'clock in the morning found Glen driving down the long dark highway. Exhausted. "Aint Nothing but a Party" pumped through the new Crutchfield quad speakers he had installed the week before. This was the first time he heard the clarity of the woofers. The boys had fallen asleep as soon as the truck door closed. It was the Gap Band and Crutchfield that kept him awake for the long ride home.

Morning light came quick. The boys had slept all night fully clothed atop the bedcovers. Nine o'clock. Melanie, the young girl from next door, reluctantly agreed to watch the boys while Glen went to his office to pick up more work. He had decided he liked spending time with his boys and would work from home the rest of the week. He was experiencing fatherhood in a new light. He was in total control and further decided it wasn't hard running the household. *Tamara complained too much.*

Nine-thirty. Hakim and Bashir were wide-awake. Breakfast was past due. Bashir never missed breakfast. "Where's our Daddy?"

Melanie lay comfortable on the sofa watching Jerry Springer's guests expose. She ignored him. They had played a fun game of horse basketball together just two days before. Now he was a nuisance.

"MELANIE!,"

"What, child."

Where is my daddy?"

"I don't know," she said without looking away from the television.

"Well, what are you doing in our house if you don't know where my daddy is?" Bashir asked.

"Trying to watch television, so back up off me."

Hakim sat on the sofa close to Melanie's bare feet. She sensed that he would try to tickle them

"Get away from my toes, Hakim," she yelled while sitting up straight.

He sat back on the cushion. His feet dangled high off the floor. With arms folded and lips poked, he whined, "I'm hungry."

"Me too," Bashir added.

Their hungry stares persuaded Melanie. "Okay okay! Go take a bath." She took her getting to the kitchen, "I'll see what's in here to eat."

It was noon before Glen returned with Sub-sandwiches and soda. Melanie was annoyed. "How much do I owe you, Mel? Glen asked, trying to mend the damage.

"Fifteen dollars."

He handed her a twenty-dollar bill, hoping that would smooth things over for the next time he needed a quick sitter.

"Thanks, Mr. Williams. When will Miss Tam be back?"

"The end of the week." He walked Mel to the back door. "Thanks for your help."

"No prob, Mr. Williams."

He was satisfied.

Lunch was over, and the boys raced to the living room. Falling to the floor, Jamal turned on the Xbox. "Who's ready to get butt whoopin'?"

Glen grabbed a game controller.

Bashir sulked. "Ah, man. I wanted to play."

"Hush up! I want to dog-out your brother. Then I'll handle you."

Jamal stretched out. "Yeah, it's on now. Give me some room."

"Okay, Jamal, kick some butt," Bashir said as he dropped down hard on the floor beside him.

"Hakim asked, "Daddy, can me and you be partners against those two."

"It's you and I. And yes.

A new relationship took hold. A brand-new door had been unlocked, and Glen could hardly wait to see what was behind it. In all the years Glen and Tamara were married, they had never done those things that were unnecessary. Those little-unplanned activities that make for warm memories. Glen wasn't charging Tamara with this neglect. He wasn't even charging himself. It was just the way it was. Stuff had to be done. He had forgotten that stuff could be fun, too.

Jamal shouted, "Rematch?"

♀

The shrilling sound of the phone ringing woke Tamara to an instant headache. All signs of Paul were gone. She was alone. The room had been cleaned. No signs of infidelity lingered. There were no leftover Reubens. No empty wine bottles or dirty glasses. No soiled towels on the bathroom floor. No crumpled trousers haphazardly tossed on the dresser or size twelve shoes hiding under a starched white shirt by the closet door. It was just Tamara and her nakedness. The television was on, but the volume had been turned down. The bed covers were on the bed neatly tucked. Had Tuesday morning been all a dream? Even if Monday wasn't, she could handle that. There was Zinfandel. Tuesday morning must have been a dream.

I had food poisoning, which caused a high fever and the high fever caused the nightmares! And that's why my head aches! Yeah! Those Reubens! They must have had bad meat. That's right! "Whew!" Tamara sighed in relief.

She let the phone ring out. High on the thought of her salvation that she would not be going to hell. She made one mistake. God will forgive her. However, there was no food poisoning. No bad meat. The phone rang again. This time she wasn't startled. She wasn't anxious to answer it either. It could be Paul. She wasn't ready to face that rancid reality. Maybe it's Glen and the boys. She surely wasn't ready for that guilt. Her sister could be calling to cancel her trip. That would suit her. She was ready to return home, anyway. She had done enough damage in that city. The conference wasn't over, but she couldn't face the young woman who was with Paul on Monday. Tamara didn't know her. It seemed that woman knew Paul well. Tamara could always tell when a woman *knew* Paul well. They rather hang in his atmosphere, like he's the center of a universe and they rotate around him, being sucked in by his gravity. And when he's done with them, he releases the hold, and they're let loose into a dark abyss. Whirling in infinite emptiness until he decides to suck them back in again.

The ringing continued. She didn't know if the ringing was one persistent caller or a series of callers. Tamara turned over and wrapped the warm pillow around the back of her head until it covered both ears. She closed her eyes. *That'll make the ringing go away.* The faint, muffled vibration annoyed her. She took the receiver from the ringing phone and placed it gently on the night table.

♂

"Hello, hello, hello… No one's there, Daddy."

"Hang up, Jamal. We'll call her back later."

♀

The train going back home seemed to take longer than the one coming. Yet, the relaxation Tamara enjoyed on her trek to New York had departed. It rained almost the entire trip, with short bouts of sunshine emerging along the way. She had hoped the rain would persuade her to sleep. It didn't. She hadn't slept since Tuesday. The cities, the towns she had passed on her way to New York, no longer seized her curiosity. She thought about her sisters and her mama; her big old house that stood in the middle of the small city, with its squeaky floorboards and dripping faucets. The pine bugs that crawled on her ceiling after midnight when she had lain wide-awake became her inspiration. No more sorrow. No protest. The grumbling ended on the ride home.

The infidelity didn't plague her mind, either. It hadn't caused her shame. She had resolved that ghost in her mind. *God is a forgiving God.* However, a subtler humiliation came that Wednesday morning. She was on her way to Penn Station when the devil-incarnate called to her. Tamara ignored him as she hurried through the traffic, darting between automobiles with her luggage in tow.

"Tam!" Paul yelled. "Wait up!"

As she turned to see if he was following her, Tamara noticed herself in the light of the day's sun. Through a storefront window, she saw herself. Eyes swollen and red; face pale and absent of any makeup. A ponytail revealed the kinky edges of her hairline. Literally and figuratively, she had been ridden hard and put up wet. Tamara stopped again briefly to peer at the woman who only days earlier had not shown her thirty-four years, let alone that advanced state of decay.

Thank God, she thought. *He didn't follow me.* In an awkward attempt to board the descending escalator, Tamara fell down face first on the gliding steps. The suitcases that were neatly tied together on a rolling cart tumbled alongside her. A woman dressed in clothes that appeared to be those of a security guard, rushed down the stairs to rescue Tamara from pain and embarrassment. There she was stretched out with a bruised forehead and matching palms, all but motionless at the bottom step, one foot on the moving stair. *Plunk, Plunk, Plunk.*

Through the people riding down the escalator, Tamara saw Paul staring down at her. Without words or expression, he turned and walked back out on the streets of New York, where by now she was convinced she had spent a holiday in hell. To her chagrin, Tamara found that New Yorkers were not all gruff and dispassionate, as she'd grown up believing. Nevertheless, if she needed that unemotional paradigm of the city as instant karma (kismet), for the sins she'd committed, then, the fall, the bumps, and the bruises were payment.

Oh God let this be my payment for my sins . . . She implored a prayer of absolution for the first time in more years than she remembered . . . *Lord, please use this as time served.*

Tamara returned to her life with Glen and the boys. No more complaints. She would be a better wife and mother. New York was a dream gone by, and she tried never to think about it again.

They have eyes full of adultery, insatiable for sin. They entice unsteady souls ... **2 Peter 2:14**

A Note from the Author

I hope you enjoyed reading Reflections in a Faded Mirror, my short stories from the Deep South. An honest effort went into the creation of every story, every character, every plot, every ending. I find pleasure in knowing that my readers frequently ask when my next book is coming out. I try to oblige by writing whenever possible and hope to have a new book coming soon.

I read somewhere that the best history lesson one can get is listening to someone who has lived it. Over the years, I've had all these stories in my head - stories from conversations with my Grandma Nita, Mama and Daddy, Aunt Lillian and Uncle Dime, my other uncles and aunts, who've long since passed away. Older co-workers of varying backgrounds have shared tales of love and of woe. Even senior members of my church have told fascinating accounts of their southern experiences. Some of these delightful stories are delicately written on the pages of my books, but all of them are forever etched in my heart.

Peace and blessings!
Toretha Wright

Other Books by the Author

Other books by the author include *Ties That Bind Us: Ivy's Passion, Souls on Fire, The Secrets of the Harvest, Flat Shoes II,* and *Dates and Nuts.*

To purchase these entertaining books by Toretha Wright, go to www.amazon.com

Look for her new works in traditional and eBook formats coming soon.

For information, email torethawright@gmail.com.